THE
BULLY
PATROL

Working on World Peace

A NOVEL
BY

DAVID DEWAR ROBERTS

Dedicated to and in loving memory
of my son Ahbry

Contents

Main Characters

DON SANCHEZ—Don cracked his head open skateboarding when he was fifteen and experienced a miraculous healing. He's twenty-eight now and has an incredible brain, so incredible he read the Bible one summer and understood the whole thing. He's Dave and Fonu's best friend.

FONU ALI—Fonu is a 350-pound Tongan and Afghani man. He started life as a strict Muslim, but when he was twelve he witnessed his father get trampled to death during the Hajj of 2015. He's twenty-eight now, and he paints like a master and sings like an angel. He's Don and Dave's best friend.

DAVE HETFIELD—Dave is a six-foot-three-inch very strong and fit athiest with an eye patch. He has some brain damage from an accident that occurred ten years earlier. He needs more brain surgery, but he's getting better. Dave is twenty-eight too and lives with Don and Fonu, who've been taking care of him since his accident.

ABE SEABROOKE—Abe was formerly the fattest fundamentalist preacher in town. Now, he's lost over one hundred pounds. He was extremely homophobic, until he fell into a coma after extreme fasting. That's when he had his homophobic awakening. He awakened to the fact, he truly was a homophobe.

LARRY COOLEY—Larry is a fifty-six-year-old, mixed race, shaven bald American. He bumped into Don while float meditating in the ocean. Larry seems mysteriously enlightened and joyful, and at the same time, a little bit crazy.

DONNA DAVIS—Donna is a beautiful feisty girl with a big dark septum ring in her nose. She escaped from a psycho ward and had been living on the streets until Larry rescued her.

ZOLA JACKSON—Zola is a founding member of the weight loss cult started by Don and Fonu to raise money for Dave's brain surgeries. Zola has lost over forty pounds and looks great now.

GERRY LONG—Gerry is Don, Fonu and Dave's Chinese African American flamboyant gay psychiatrist neighbor, who comes over for a beer with the boys.

CHAPTER 1

Another Bombing

Another nine-eleven bombing occurred on Earth. 1331 humans were killed instantly, many more were trapped in the rubble, buried alive and slowly dying.

～

It was mid-morning in San Jose, California when Don Sanchez heard the news. He sat on the edge of his bed and closed his eyes. He took a deep breath and let it out slowly. He was silent for several moments. He inhaled deeply and stood up. "Why?" He breathed out into the air of his room. He squeezed his eyes shut, spread his arms wide, and with his nose pointed to the ceiling cried out, "Will we ever have peace with humans still existing?"

There was no answer Don could here.

Then he heard, "Don, Don, I can't believe it. They did it again."

Don went to the kitchen to find his good friend Fonu Ali standing there making a sandwich. "They did it again Don," Fonu Ali said.

"World peace seems further away than ever brother," Don said, putting his hand on Fonu Ali's shoulder.

Dave came into the kitchen too, and the three of them watched people getting rescued on the TV news.

"People argue a lot," Don said. "Mostly, people argue about what's good and what's bad. Are we even arguing about if murdering people in the name of God is bad?"

Dave and Fonu Ali just shook their heads.

⁓

The next day Don was float meditating in the Pacific Ocean on a beautiful warm September morning. He was focused on his breathing and drifting off to sounds of sea lions barking and seagulls squawking from their homes near the Santa Cruz wharf. The smell of ocean water and seaweed was in the air. There was no wind and very little swell. It was a perfect day to float meditate.

Don was totally at ease physically. Mentally, he was entering an altered state. The ocean cradled his body, as another part of him flew off to outer space, away from the violence of the world and into the silence of this totally relaxed place.

Don was traumatized, along with millions of people on planet Earth. He was even more traumatized by the images he saw of people rejoicing on his same planet. Yes, some people on planet Earth rejoiced and thanked God while other people, trapped and buried, were dying.

The funny part was, on planet Earth, many people did not believe in evil at all.

~

Don Sanchez was searching for an answer to the seemingly impossible problem of achieving world peace. He thought about how he could help, what he could do, and why he was here on Earth. Don thought about God too, and even though he was raised by Buddhist professors who did not believe in God, Don believed in the supernatural. You see, Don had experienced a miracle.

CHAPTER 2

Dreams

When Don was fifteen, he crashed on his skateboard and cracked his head open. Somehow, during the healing process, after all the rewiring, Don received an exceptionally good brain after his exceptionally bad crash. The doctors couldn't explain it. They just said, "Somebody up there must like this kid."

Don started having amazing dreams. He dreamed of playing the piano as easily as he could hum his favorite tune. He dreamed of playing the trumpet too, and in his dreams his lips never got tired. In his dreams, Don had a complete understanding of all the depths of music. Sometimes when he woke up, he wanted to go back to sleep, his dreams were so good.

Don dreamed of animals too. He dreamed he was a bear, catching salmon with his hands in the river. He dreamed of talking to bears, and in his dreams, the bears talked too. The bears told Don they would protect him. So, he should be brave. And even though he couldn't see them when he was awake, they were there right beside him, and he would always be safe.

His dreams taught him to have confidence. He learned there was plenty of time to learn new things. He knew he could learn to play music. He knew it without a doubt. So, first he picked up the harmonica, and later he taught himself piano.

Don had so many interests, he sometimes struggled with what to spend his time on. He grew up believing hard work was the answer to everything, but Don Sanchez wanted to understand more. He wanted to understand where his dreams came from. Were they from some ancient musical relative, passed down in his genes or cells or something? Or, maybe it was reincarnation? Maybe he was a trumpet player or a bear in a past life? Reincarnation might explain some of his cool dreams.

Don thought dreams might be communication with God. He knew communication was good. Therefore, communication with God must be beyond good. It must be incredible, like playing piano in a dream without thinking. And if communication with God was really possible, Don certainly had questions.

CHAPTER 3

Loud Christians, Quiet Buddhists

Don Sanchez had questions about religion. He wanted to know why some Christians were such know-it-all's and so certain reincarnation wasn't true. And he thought it was rude when he heard someone refer to another person's belief as a false religion. Don noticed that offensive words were powerful enough to stop communication, and he knew that, without communication, problems would not get solved. Therefore, Don knew that words offending another person's belief were bad, because they stopped communication.

Don also noticed that belief was very powerful, even belief in something that was not true. He learned this by observing people believing in things that were not true. Don saw people all around him believing that money or the perfect spouse, was all they needed for happiness, and from his observations, he knew this was not true. Mostly, Don saw people leaving out the supernatural.

But Don was thinking beyond the material world. Don Sanchez wanted to believe in only what was true, one hundred percent true. So, he studied a lot. He studied math, chemistry and physics. He studied the Bible, the Quran and the Bhagavad Gita. He studied people and philosophy. Don was a student of everything, but mostly, it was his dreams and meditation that fascinated him.

The Zen Buddhist teaching that, at some point, one could accomplish everything by doing nothing, especially fascinated him. At first it made no sense, being raised by such driven, hard working parents. *How could anyone accomplish anything by doing nothing?*

———

Don was always impressed by his father trying to remember the names of everyone he met. The delivery guys and gals, the homeless regulars near the drug store, the mail carriers and neighbors walking by, people working at the supermarket, people he only met one time, Don's father tried to remember everyone's name, and Don thought it was very cool.

Before a get together, Don's father worked on the names of all the people coming over. He made a list, trying to remember the names of all his distant relatives and everyone's kids. When he couldn't remember a name, he would say, "Nope, it's not coming to me, gotta let it go, next subject please." Don's father would purposely stop trying to remember, and then later, the name would suddenly pop into his head. And Don took notice of this.

As Don got older, he learned it was similar with meditation. Don learned he could drop questions into the silence and then forget about them. Later, the answers would come. It might be the next day, or the next night in his dreams. Or, it might be the next week paddling to catch a wave, an answer would suddenly pop into his head. And Don was fascinated by this.

Don wondered if meditation was like praying. He wondered if it was God giving him the answers, or just his incredible brain. In meditation, Don found answers with his eyes closed, without even moving or even trying. For Don, meditation was just asking and relaxing. Later, the answers would come. His favorite form of meditation was floating in the ocean. In this form of meditation, he did move a little. He drifted, and he bobbed.

CHAPTER 4

Float Meditating in the Pacific

Today, Don was float meditating in the Pacific Ocean. He was on his back breathing smoothly. He was again dropping the world peace question into the sea of tranquility, and then forgetting about it. Don was in a deep meditative state. It was kind of like sleeping, but he was not sleeping. It was kind of like dreaming, but he was not dreaming. Don was totally tranced out leashed to the big blue surfboard floating next to him. Then, he bumped into something. "What the hell!" Don exclaimed, as he reeled back in from outer space.

"I thought you were a shark. You scared the crap out of me," Larry said, as he climbed up on his board.

"Where did you come from man?" Don said, now straddling his board too with his palms on his thighs.

"I was floating," Larry said. "Sorry, I was kind of tranced out."

"I was floating too man! I was way out there!" Don said. "You've got to be kidding me. What are the odds? Both completely tranced out, floating in the ocean, and then bumping into each other? Anyway, it's always nice to meet another floater." Don extended his hand with a big smile. "My name is Don Sanchez, and I am very glad you're not a shark."

"Same here Don. It's good to meet you too. My name is Larry Cooley and there are no odds for something like this."

"I know man! It's gotta be God or something," Don said, with his eyes wide open and most of his fingers pointing to the sky.

"Really? God?" Larry asked, kind of surprised. "You don't hear much about God nowadays, especially from serious Buddhist meditators."

"That's correct, you won't hear much about God from Buddhists," Don said. "But one thing's for certain, if everyone was a true Buddhist, killing and harming others would stop. True Buddhists don't even hurt cockroaches. If everyone was a true Buddhist, war would end, we would have world peace, and a lot of over-weight Americans might become mindful about their eating. The question is, how do you know if anyone's a true anything, unless you know what they're thinking? What about you Larry, are you a true anything?"

"What?" Larry replied. "You want to know my spiritual belief?"

"Sure," Don said. "I study the supernatural. And hell, we just bumped into each other floating in the ocean. So, I'd love to hear why you believe how you believe."

"Okay, well, since you asked me, I'll tell you," Larry said. "I'm trying to be a follower of what Jesus taught, and I'm okay with gay marriage. I need to start off with a brief gay acceptance speech, because I believe the church at large doesn't have a good answer for a gay person. And they keep repeating the same bad answers, so for me, I'll leave the whole gay thing up to God, because I was born straight."

"A follower of what Jesus taught," Don said, thinking and rubbing his chin.

"What about you Don? Are you a true anything? A true Buddhist perhaps?"

"I'm not much for labels," Don said. "But I like the Buddha's example of walking away from organized religion. Even though he was a rich, high class Hindu, he knew it was wrong to look down on other people. I like that the Buddha was especially mindful of his thoughts. He didn't like having bad thoughts of other people, and neither do I.

"I grew up with Buddha statues, and I'm really into meditation, nature and the whole Zen thing, so I'm truly part Buddhist. But man, I need to add to it because I believe in miracles and the supernatural. I need more than just Buddhist teachings. I need a bigger purpose than doing karmic good deeds and searching for enlightenment in the silence, sitting in a cave or something, trying to think of nothing, meditating all day. I can't label myself a true Buddhist because that would be too limiting. I've studied it, and I believe it's part of the big story. I've studied the Bhagavad Gita, the Bible and the Quran too. You see, I study what people argue about, and at this point I'm not taking sides. If I ever choose to take sides, I'll side with the people being bullied."

"That sounds like a mentally healthy belief," Larry said.

"Mental health is one of my big goals," Don said. "I'm trying to find some sanity in a world full of religious crazy people. One side killing people in the name of God, and the other side bullying people in the name of God."

"I know, the super religious can make sane people want to become atheist," Larry said.

"Yea, I know, but I can't be atheist," Don said. Then he smiled and raised his voice and said, "Because I believe in miracles!"

Larry looked at Don beaming. Don was a beautiful, alive human being. "But, I've never met an atheist I didn't like," Don said. "My best friend Dave's an atheist, and he's the friendliest and most well-tempered person I've ever met. I don't think Dave ever has a bad thought or a bad day anymore. But then again, Dave has some brain damage, so Dave's in the special category."

"Oh, I remember when I was a young atheist," Larry said, reflecting back to his college days. "I sure did what seemed to be right in my own eyes, that's for sure."

"That's from the book of Judges in the Bible," Don said, putting his hands on his thighs and looking Larry intensely in the eyes. "Not many people quote the Bible in everyday conversation. Are you a Bible bumper Larry?" Don asked, laughing a little.

"I try to understand it more than combine it with politics and force feed it to others," Larry said. "And from my experience it's true, people do what seems to be right in their own eyes. It's one of the main themes from the Bible. It means people like to come up with their own theories."

"You're right about that," Don said. "My friend Fonu Ali and I have a theory. Okay, you seem cool enough with your gay marriage disclaimer and all. It just seems strange hearing someone quote the Bible."

"It's surprising to me a young meditator like you knew I was quoting the Bible," Larry said. "Most people push away the supernatural and the sacred. Most people have been taught that religions and religious people were the problem in the world. So, why study what they read?"

"Yes, one could say that religion is the problem and religion is the answer," Don said. "Or that no religion is the problem and no religion is the answer. I think we need to redefine what the word religion means. If religion means believing in God, I believe God is the answer. If religion means believing some large organization's doctrine is flawless, I believe religion is the problem. I also think we need to redefine what the word Christian means, because some of what comes to mind, besides what Jesus taught, isn't too attractive."

"Yes, we definitely need to change religion," Larry said, "rather than eliminating God from the equation."

"Somehow, we need to eliminate money from the equation instead," Don said, "and the power and temptation that go with it."

"That sure would be a big goal," Larry said.

CHAPTER 5

Muhammad Had a Point

"Speaking of big goals," Don said, with his arms raised like a football goal had just been made. "The answer finally came to me! The answer to my biggest goal."

"What big goal is that?" Larry replied.

"World peace man! I've been working on it for six years now..." Then Don paused and said, "Actually, I've only been meditating on it. It all started after the bombings and fires of 2025. At the time, it sounded like a good idea to work on the world peace problem. After a lot of thought, I concluded religions were at the root of the world peace problem. Then I got depressed, because how could one person change religion? Thinking about it gave me a massive headache, so I had to stop. I had to drop the world peace question into the sea of tranquility and then forget about it. Well, today the answer hit me about the same time you did Larry."

"The answer to world peace?" Larry asked. *Is this guy serious?*

"Yes," Don said, with certainty in his voice. "At least, I think it has a lot to do with it. What I came back with was, Muhammad had a point!"

"What? You mean the Muslim Muhammad?" Larry asked. "The guy who dictated the Quran?"

"Yes, the Muslim Muhammad," Don replied. And then he repeated, "Muhammad had a point," as he closed his eyes. Don was in deep thought putting together the pieces of the world peace puzzle. "Actually Larry, Muhammad had several points, but the one I'm referring to is his point about the Trinity being so confusing. Yes, Muhammad had a point. The Trinity is confusing. But why throw out the *Sermon on the Mount*, that's what I can't figure out? Yes, Muhammad had a point! But why did he throw out the radical idea of loving your enemies?" Don's speech slowed and got very deliberate, "Yes, I can admit Muhammad had a point, and at the same time disagree with his entire theory."

"Yes, I know, the Trinity can be confusing," Larry said.

"And with all the statues and the ring kissing, if I really try, I can feel Muhammad," Don said. "But why would he say Jesus didn't die on the cross? That's what I can't figure out, because Jesus laying down his life on the cross was the perfect ending to the Bible story I read. It was totally obvious to me, especially since they never found his body and the guards never broke his legs. Throwing out the *Sermon on the Mount* was like throwing out something really good.

"Just think if the Pope could admit Muhammad had a point and the Grand Islamic Ayatollah could admit the *Sermon on the Mount* was sacred?" Don paused to think.

Then he got a big smile on his face and exclaimed, "World peace! It's possible man. Ah ha," Don laughed, snorted and slapped the water.

"Muhammad was confused about the Trinity, and he thought the Catholic statues were like idol worship, right?"

"That's my understanding," Larry replied.

"I'm sure he talked with his local priest about it," Don said, "And I'm sure he hit a brick wall too, because the Pope and his priests really like statues. I'm sure Muhammad asked himself at the time, 'How could one person change religion?' I see it so clearly now. It all makes sense."

"What makes sense?" Larry asked.

"Muhammad's whole life," Don replied. "You know, how the Muslim religion got started. Check it out. Muhammad's wife was a very wealthy widow who really loved him, and Muhammad was a very special man. Of course she wanted him to be happy, but Muhammad was very sad. He was sad because the Pope wouldn't admit the Trinity was confusing, or that praying to statues of saints might possibly be bad.

"Muhammad's wife was not only wealthy, she was brilliant, and she had a good idea! Rather than try to change Catholic doctrine, she suggested it might be easier to start an entirely new religion. Her idea really got Muhammad's attention. He immediately perked up and came out of his depression. He was fascinated by his wife's good idea. They both got excited and quickly went to work.

"They hired a dream team of Jewish lawyers and Bible experts, formed a think tank, and centered their new religion around the Old Testament Bible story along with Muhammad's valid points."

"Your theory suggests Jewish lawyers wrote the Quran?" Larry asked.

"Who else?" Don replied in a Yiddish accent, shrugging his shoulders with his palms to the sky. "They've always been the smartest people in the world, not to mention Old Testament Bible experts.

"And the Jewish lawyers they hired were truly artists. They were geniuses. They were perfect for the job. They called their new book the Holy Quran, or The Recitation from God. This time, the Arabic people would be God's chosen ones, not the Jews. This time, Jesus wouldn't die on the cross to complete God's story of love. This time, Muhammad would be the final prophet. And the cherry on top, they turned the entire story into a beautiful hypnotic song, perfect for brainwashing someone. That is, when it was sung in Arabic, the language of God's newest chosen ones.

Don was speaking with his eyes closed, "Muhammad and his wife loved it! They loved that it was made into a beautiful song. They loved that they made the Arabic people God's chosen ones. They thought it was only fair. They thought it was pure genius. The problem was, they were humans with no idea of what a truly good idea was. So, after Muhammad died, his relatives scrambled for control, and they've been fighting about it ever since."

After a while only listening and thinking Larry said, "So, it would be better to come together and take what's good from all religions, including Muhammad's valid points, and communicate, rather than run for cover and toss bombs at each other?"

"Yes," Don said. "And finding the good requires learning what each other's sacred scripture teaches. Christians and atheists need to read the Quran, and Muslims and Jews need to read the New Testament. Then everyone should vote on what should be termed sacred and what should be termed troublesome. We should let regular people decide, instead of old men in robes, which was one of Muhammad's valid points. He pointed out that holy clergy in their holy robes were not necessary. The one's at the top were actually part of the problem, and I agree."

"Imagine a Muslim reading the *Sermon on the Mount* for the first time," Larry said.

"They might get woken up to the way they were brainwashed growing up," Don said. "Ideas like loving and praying for their enemies would surely be mind blowing."

"You like the *Sermon on the Mount* too?" Larry asked. "Are you a Christian Don?"

"Nope. Stop right there!" Don exclaimed. "Please don't put the Christian label on me. Let me explain. I have a problem with that label, because God wouldn't want us to teach only ninety-nine percent of the truth. You know, one percent error can cause a whole lot of insanity. Yes, I love the *Sermon on the Mount*, but I can't accept the Christian label. Not now. Not today. I feel it would be like taking sides with the bully in the schoolyard calling somebody else's little kid a fag, and I'm not going to do it. I know that would be bad."

"That's why I'm a closet Christian," Larry said. "Well, until someone asks me like you did."

"That's smart," Don said. "So, what do you think about Muhammad possibly having a point."

"Okay," Larry replied. "Let me repeat what I think I just heard. You said Muhammad had a point regarding the Holy Trinity being confusing for a lot of people."

"Yes," Don said.

"And, I'm sure he had something to say about the holy water, and of course, the blessed crackers."

"Yes, and the blessed crackers we're talking about aren't the white dudes in robes," Don said, with a big smile.

"Yes, I know," Larry said, laughing. "The Catholic blessed crackers are the only blessed crackers that actually become human flesh when put on your tongue by a holy priest. It's pretty obvious, the Catholics tried to corner the market on God."

"Why do there have to be a holy middle men between us and God?" Don asked.

"Because there's a lot of money involved," Larry replied. "A pastor once told me, if I really wanted to experience the Lord, I needed to start giving ten percent of my income to the church. When I suggested giving five percent to the church and five percent to the Special Olympics, he said ten percent of my gross income was the proper offering to the church. He would give it to God. That was how it worked."

"Man," Don said. "I'm sure the priests told Muhammad the same thing they told aboriginal people all over the world. Somehow, the priests were blessed with the gift of explaining to people living on tree bark and crickets what ten percent of their gross income was."

Larry laughed and said, "If I lived in Muhammad's time and the church refused to translate the Bible into Arabic, that sure would've made me mad. I agree, Muhammad had a point. Personally, I'm suspicious of men who wear robes at work, promise they'll never have sex again, and make their living hearing people's confessions and nasty thoughts, not to mention the ring kissing and silly hats. It's kind of medieval."

"They treat their doctrine like God himself," Don said. "They can't admit the possibility they might be wrong about the wickedness of contraception, because they're afraid they'll lose the control they wielded with their holy doctrine.

"They don't understand, it's better to be truthful and admit error and the possibility of error. It's so much better than spreading insanity. But they can't understand because they're thinking like military commanders, who can't admit doubt. Imagine a military commander admitting doubt to their troops, admitting they might possibly be wrong about killing the other side. Immediately, I tell you, the fighting would stop. The troops would talk, and the commander would lose control.

"What about you Larry?" Don said with a serious look. "You said you were a follower of what Jesus taught. How do you explain your belief when you disagree with the people at the top?"

"I don't need the people at the top," Larry replied. "I believe Jesus came to Earth to complete God's story of love played out in human form. I believe God sent us messages through people's life stories, that are now in the Bible. And yes, I believe the Bible is supernatural, but before you label me a brainwashed bible bumper who only reads one book, just know, I have my own theory too.

"I believe gay acceptance on one extreme and Bible acceptance on the other extreme can be achieved if we all realize the Bible was written from the hardwired hetero-sexual male point of view. So, if you're a hardwired hetero-sexual man, it makes perfect sense. If you're a gay person or an independent woman, just realize, some things need to be reinterpreted. This is where I diverge from the loud and powerful Christians at the top, like the ones on radio and television."

"God's story played out in human form," Don repeated, as he pondered the depth of what this meant.

"Yes Don," Larry replied.

"So," Don said, pausing to think. "When Jesus said, 'It is finished' as he died on the cross, it was the conclusion of God's story, even though the New Testament Bible hadn't been written yet."

"Exactly," Larry said.

"I like that," Don said. "So, the perfect inerrant story of God's love was indeed perfect and inerrant as it was played out in human form," Don paused to think.

"Yes, and then fallible humans..." Larry said, waiting for Don to get it.

"Wrote it down," Don said, completing Larry's sentence.

"Yes," Larry said. "And today, two thousand plus years later, people are still arguing about the end of the story. The Jewish leaders didn't like the end of the story, because they requested the death of their own savior.

"The Arabic men didn't like the end of the story either, because it put the Catholics in power, and the pope said they could only have one wife. So, the Arabic men accused the Catholics of inserting things into God's story they didn't like."

"I like this," Don said. "So, people can believe in the perfect story of God's love, straight from God, without having to accept and believe every word, doctrine and interpretation written by humans."

"Exactly," Larry said. "Psalms nineteen says God's story was written in the stars when the universe was formed. I think the ancient Shamans could interpret the stars directly and tell their own stories to help people get through life and realize how much God loves them. Later, the stories came alive in human beings at the time, directed by angels or something. And then even later, other people wrote it down."

"It's funny," Don said. "You said we humans like to come up with our own theories and do what seems right in our own eyes."

"Yes, it's one of the main themes from the Bible," Larry said.

"My friend Fonu Ali and I have a theory."

CHAPTER 6

Don and Fonu's World Peace Theory

"We have a world peace theory," Don said. "Once we all can admit the possibility we might be one percent wrong, that's all we need to achieve world peace. And when I say we all, I mean everyone, Jewish and Muslim, capitalist and communist, Catholic and Protestant, atheists and of course all parents. Everyone who can't admit this possibility should look in the mirror, because they need therapy."

"I think you're onto something," Larry said. "Fonu Ali? That's an interesting name. You and Fonu came up with this theory?

"Yes, it's part of our overall inner peace theory," Don said.

"Is it because of all the terror attacks lately?"

"Yes, in a way," Don said. "But really, it all started because my friend Fonu Ali was born a Muslim and his father got trampled to death during the Hajj of 2015. You know, the Islamic pilgrimage to Mecca?"

"Yes, of course, I know the Hajj," Larry replied, "required of all good, healthy Muslims once in a lifetime. Your friend's father got trampled to death during the Hajj?"

"Yes, Fonu was only twelve at the time. It was a miracle he survived," Don said. "The death of Fonu's father had a huge effect on him, as one might expect. And Fonu Ali has had a huge effect on me. And now, we're talking along the lines of the same thing."

"Wow, your friend Fonu must have a story to tell."

"Yes, he certainly does," Don said. "Fonu Ali was raised a strict Muslim, and he loved his father a lot. When he saw him get trampled to death before his eyes, he was severely traumatized. Mostly, he wanted to understand why he survived. Well, you know how our greatest gifts can result from our worst tragedies?"

"Yes, I believe it," Larry replied.

"Fonu's gift became a passion for studying all religions. First of all, he wanted to figure out why a loving God would want people to go on the Hajj pilgrimage. It can reach 108 degrees or more out there, and they were poor and couldn't afford it. Fonu tried his hardest to understand why his father, or anyone for that matter, would want to go to the exact same place, at the exact same time, as millions of other hot, sweaty people."

"Sounds like Fonu was shaken awake by his tragedy," Larry said.

"That's for sure," Don said. "Fonu was shaken awake to the possibility that how he believed was at least one percent in error, and he wanted to know the truth, and so did I. That's what led to our good friendship and our theory. It seemed to us, the big problems in the world always involved the big organized religions. So, we studied the religions and we talked, and we thought a lot about it, until finally, we came up with our theory. We call it, *The Insertion Theory*.

"*The Insertion Theory* is our theory that well-meaning men inserted words, verses, and possibly even entire books of sacred scripture. And because of these insertions, both the Quran and the Bible could be at least one percent in error. The problem is, each religion insists their book is the perfect one. Therefore, our culture is at war with the religious and throwing out everything sacred.

"In our theory, rather than throw out the sacred books, we suggest de-inserting the possibly inserted verses. Like Quranic verses teaching Muslims to think bad thoughts about Christians and Jews and other people who don't believe like they do. Or, like Biblical verses teaching Christians to think bad thoughts of gay people. We like to think of the Bible and other sacred scripture more like a buffet, avoiding the offensive items possibly inserted by man, and only choosing what is good."

"A theory that includes the Bible," Larry said. "That's rare."

"It sounds like you've studied your Bible pretty thoroughly," Don said.

"Yes, and I've thought a lot about it too," Larry replied.

"I can't believe I bumped into a Bible bumper out floating in the ocean," Don said, laughing.

"I'm not a Bible bumper Don! Don't forget, you asked me what I believed!" Larry said, getting a little defensive. "You asked me! So, I told you! Please don't label me a brainwashed Bible bumper until you get to know me. Today, I'm a closet Christian. Well, unless you ask me, then I'll tell you. I learned my lesson. I don't say anything about my beliefs, until I've been asked. I study the Bible looking for the big themes, because I want the big understanding. And I think I found it, but I don't mention the Bible anymore. I realized most people take it wrong, because it conflicts with their theory.

"People tend to put Bible believers like me in a box, before they learn I have some real concerns about large organized religions too. For example, Jesus taught us to eat with others, not just with people who believe exactly how we do. Jesus taught us to love our neighbors, by breaking bread with them. It's hard to believe He meant for it to become a church ritual with sacred crackers and certified priest's, only for those in a state of grace. If that was the case, there should be no one in line."

"The church is just doing what seems to be right in its own eyes," Don said. "The problem is the money, because the money turns the church into a business. It shouldn't be a business, but as a business religions want a monopoly, and they want more members. So, they demonize contraception and deny over population exists. As a business, they aren't concerned with the extinction of species, and they don't really care about gay people, since they don't breed and have huge families. And they don't dare consider their infallible message might bring insanity to the small gay minority who are in love and want to be married."

"When it comes to organized religions, I think we're in violent agreement," Larry said.

"Sorry about that Bible Bumper jab," Don said. "I can see you're not into labels either."

"No, I'm not," Larry replied. "A label doesn't prove anyone's a true anything. What I learned was, people will believe all sorts of things as long as they still believe they're basically good compared to others around them. Most people don't understand, they shouldn't compare themselves with others, because God makes people very, very different."

"You're right about that," Don said. "Some people have been blessed with good everything, good nutrition, good parents, good schools, good intelligence, not to mention good brainwashing. Other people, it seems, have been cursed with bad everything, like a kidnapped child raised by pirates. Therefore, a direct comparison is not valid."

CHAPTER 7

Mirror of Badness

"Seemingly cursed people can end up more blessed than seemingly blessed people," Larry said, with a big smile. "That is, if we wake up before we kill ourselves or someone else. Yes, like a kidnapped child raised by pirates or just a very dysfunctional parent, we can end up with lots of problems. We like drinking or doing drugs too much, or too much sex, and anything but moderation. For us, the skids of sin were well greased, and we went down to the bottom fast.

"The blessing is!" Larry said enthusiastically, like being on the bottom was a good thing, "from the bottom, our mirror of badness becomes crystal clear. From the bottom, we can see ourselves and our world differently. From the bottom, with the scales of pride off our eyes, the Bible can now be understood, like a blind person seeing, at least that's how it was for me.

"It's a lot harder for a seemingly blessed person, like someone from a seemingly normal family that's got it made, to see their need for change, so in a way, they're blind. It's another big theme from the Bible. A lot of rich, successful people are blind to the mysteries of God, so in a way, they're cursed."

"I had good parents and a great childhood," Don said. "Do you think I'm cursed because I won't admit I'm a screwed-up sinner?"

"Of course, your good parents were a blessing," Larry said, "but getting back to your Bible bumper quip. Do you really think all Christians are the same? Why would you think that? And why would you call me a Bible bumper so quickly? How many Bible bumpers do you know who have studied the Quran and the Bhagavad Gita?"

"Not a single one. Sorry Larry," Don said, extending his hand to mend the fence.

Don thought about his parents as they shook hands. "Mirror of Badness eh?" Don said, as he contemplated deeply what it meant. "You're talking about original sin, the first big theme from the Bible."

"Yes!" Larry exclaimed, with a surprised look on his face, slapping the water with both hands. Larry didn't know about Don's incredible brain. Larry didn't know Don cracked his head open when he was fifteen and had a miraculous healing. Larry didn't know Don's brain healed much better than before. He didn't know Don read the entire Bible one summer, when he was eighteen, and he understood the whole thing.

"Yes, I read the Bible," Don said. "I understand original sin as the bad thoughts that seem to pop into my head now and then. I think the biggest theme of the Bible is the promise that, if we think of others first, we'll end up in the joyful place up here," Don said, putting his index finger to his head. "So, I try to do that."

"Wow Don!" Larry exclaimed. "It sounds like you really get it. That's a beautiful description of the overall main theme, and you did it without even mentioning Jesus' name. Maybe you're a reincarnated shaman who used to read the stars?"

"I don't think so," Don said. "You wouldn't say that if you knew the thoughts popping into my head. My thoughts convict me, but regarding my actions, I try to do more good and stay away from hurtful words. I don't think of myself as all that bad of a filthy rag or wicked person who needs to be saved from hell's inferno."

"Now, you're quoting the Bible!" Larry exclaimed. He was amazed. Don seemed to really know the Bible. "That's Isaiah 64:6, 'All our righteous acts are like filthy rags.' I know how difficult it is when you're young and feeling immortal to see yourself as a filthy rag or bad enough to justify joining some religion."

"I don't," Don said confidently. "Like I said, I read the Bible. And I believe in miracles. And with world peace as my biggest goal, I especially studied the Old Testament books of Isaiah, Psalms and the books of Moses, because the Muslims, Christians and Jews all agree they're supernatural. Once I learned these three religions actually agreed on something, of course I studied these books. But I don't feel like a dirty rotten sinner or all that bad of a person."

"That's great," Larry said. "All I can say is, just keep on being good. You're young. Enjoy your life. I'm just happy you know the message. So, if ever there comes a time when you look in the mirror, and feel bad or stuck in a pit, like you need to be rescued or something, always remember you can ask God for help. It's a sign of strength, not weakness."

Don was thinking about Larry's theory, "You said God's story was written in the stars and then played out in human form before the Bible was ever written."

"Yes Don."

"It just hit me," Don said. "Both our theories address the inerrancy problem, which has always bugged the crap out of me. Why does every word in some holy book have to be perfect, God breathed and error free, when it doesn't have to be? We can still get the main themes. What, is there some new cool church in Santa Cruz teaching this stuff?"

"Cool Church, here in Santa Cruz?" Larry said. "I don't know about that. I'm from San Jose. *Mirror of Badness* is the title of a book I'm working on, and God's story written in the stars is described in Psalms 19. It's not my theory. I don't attend Church anymore," Larry said, lowering his head. "There's no cool church in Santa Cruz or anywhere that I know of. I've been studying a lot on my own and meditating and praying a lot too, trying to figure it all out. You know, find the whole truth. I used to go to church, but then my life got turned upside down."

"Really? What happened?" Don asked.

"My wife left me for a woman," Larry replied.

"Oh, sorry to hear that man," Don said.

"It's okay," Larry said. "The crushing helped me under-stand my insides more. I learned a lot. It's been ten years now, and I've changed for the better."

"You've got the right attitude," Don said, looking Larry straight in the eyes. Don's look showed he really understood. "It didn't turn you into a raging homophobe did it?"

"No, far from it," Larry said. "Now, I'm more like a church-o-phobe. I can't describe it without getting emotional."

"It's always good to talk about our stuff," Don said, "and crying's okay."

"I know Don," Larry said. "What really made an impres-sion on me, was when I went back to church alone. Everyone was supportive. The problem was, the support was one sided. All the church elders blamed her. They said she was dancing with her demons, and this was proof homosexuals wanted to destroy the family unit as we know it."

"Brainwashed church cats," Don said, shaking his head slowly.

"Yes, all the church cats were dumbfounded when I disagreed with them," Larry said. "I just couldn't go along with their evil gay theory and the blame they were laying. They said being with a woman was her own selfish choice, and she could change if she wanted to. They concluded our break-up was her choice too. They were pointing fingers at her like a bunch of bullies.

"At that time, I was feeling the craziness. So, I did as Socrates suggested. I examined my life. Then, I examined her life and her family's. I concluded, she married me because of her wealthy, rigid, Baptist family. She knew she'd be cut off if she ever came out. Essentially, she married me for her family's money. Her life insanity spread to me. When her parents got killed in a car accident, she was finally free to be herself. So, she left me."

"It's ironic," Don said. "Narrow-minded church teachings were really the cause of your broken family, not your gay ex-wife. I can tell you really loved her, but you two were never meant to remain together."

"Yes!" Larry exclaimed, slapping the water and making a big splash. "You got it Don! The church was really the cause of my broken family. The church and her parents pressuring her to cover up how she really felt inside. I realized, my broken dream of having a family was caused by the church's narrow teaching on the whole gay thing. The church didn't have a good answer. What the church taught didn't work for a hardwired gay person. And that's my experience with organized religion.

"So, she left me, and I got really depressed," Larry said, dropping his head. "Then I left the church, and turned to drugs, alcohol and prostitutes until I hit bottom. But that's when I had my awakening. That's when my life really started to change." Larry suddenly looked very happy. He smiled and said, "Now, everything's okay, and I'm in the happy, joyful place."

"You do seem strangely happy," Don said. "And strangely truthful, straight out the gate. I'm not surprised you can't hang with those church cats anymore. You seem pretty cool, floating and all."

"Don't get me wrong Don," Larry said. "I am a born-again believer, but I also believe the church body has a disease, eating away at it from the inside, that's not too attractive. Like the Catholic teaching that using contraception is inherently evil. Hey, I'm pro-life too, but there are exceptions. And demonizing contraception is just plain crazy.

"I get it. The Pope wants to teach us not to idolize sex, and for couples to take a break from the boning for a while each month. I get it, but what I don't get is risking a disease or an unwanted pregnancy just to keep the church's inerrant doctrine intact. That's what I think is crazy."

"Or evil?" Don said. "Are they crazy or are they evil, that is the question? It's difficult to answer this regarding people, because if you say a person is evil, you will look like the crazy one. But regarding an organization, how can an organization be crazy?"

"People can appear evil, because they have a demon inside," Larry said. "But I think the church at large is just prideful, because they can't admit the possibility they might be one percent wrong, like in your world peace theory.

"And like pedophile priests are to the Catholic Church and terrorists are to Islam, the homophobes with hot wives at my church were like a disease to me, and I had to leave," Larry said. "I had to get away for the sake of my sanity."

"Homophobes with hot wives eh?" Don said, with a big toothy grin. "You're all right Larry."

"I'm feeling some sanity here today," Larry said.

"Sanity is one of my big goals," Don said. "And considering yesterday's insane bombings, this is very consistent with my Zoroastrian dualistic belief.

"Zoroastrian?" Larry asked, thinking for a moment. "Didn't they build towers for the dead, so the birds would dispose of the bodies?"

"You've done your homework," Don said. "Yes, the ancient Zoroastrians believed in not polluting the earth, air or water, so they built towers for their dead. The bodies were picked clean, the birds were fed and all that was left was dry bones. We don't do that anymore, but the symbolism describes our strong belief in not polluting.

"We believe in good. We believe in evil. Who can argue with dualism? It's so balanced. It's so good and bad and yin and yang and all that pleasure and pain and life and death, but no one believes in evil anymore. It's just not cool. It's so much cooler to believe that God is love and evil is just the absence of love."

"Oh yes," Larry said, with a smile. "I remember believing evil was like darkness. It was nothing to fear. It was just the absence of light. Yes, it's very comforting not to believe in evil at all. It's so much easier to believe people are basically good. It's a good theory, but is it the truth?"

"My belief in God increased as I experienced evil in my own life," Don said.

"I think that's why evil exists and bad things happen," Larry said. "Because once we believe in evil, it's a whole lot easier to believe in God. You see, Satan, the prince of darkness, doesn't want us to believe in him," Larry said, growling like an animal and making horns on his head with his fingers.

"You know Larry," Don said, as he rubbed his chin and searched for the right words. "When you quote the Bible and talk about demons and Satan, you kind of come off like a Jesus freak. I'm not calling you one. I'm just saying."

"Between you and me Don, I am a Jesus freak," Larry said. "And when someone asks me, I tell them. I give 'em both barrels, because I know what I believe now. I'm not trying to be cool or trying to impress humans anymore. I say what I believe, when asked, because I believe communication holds the answer to everything."

"You know Larry," Don said. "I always believed communication held the answer to everything too."

"It's hard to be cool and be a Jesus freak," Larry said.

"That's why I'm Zoroastrian," Don said.

"Yes Don. And I'm fully pruned out," Larry said, turning his wrinkled palms up to the sky.

Don turned his palms up to the sky too. They were both thoroughly pruned out. It was time to paddle in.

CHAPTER 8

Dave

D on and Larry paddled in, talking the whole way. They rinsed their wetsuits and Don returned his board outside the surf shop near the wharf. Larry propped up his board outside the shop, and they both walked in.

"Hi Don," the pretty girl behind the counter said with an eager smile, as she ran over and jumped into Don's arms giving him a big hug. "How was your float today? I bet it was great! The conditions are perfect. It's beyond flat out there. Did you bring back anything from outer space?"

"I brought back a new friend I bumped into out there," Don said, gesturing for Larry to come over. "And, I brought back a clue to solving the world peace problem. Abbs, I'd like you to meet Larry. Larry, this is Abigail Duffey. Abbs is one of the best young surfers on the planet. Larry and I were both tranced out floating, and we literally bumped into each other out there."

"What?" Abbs said, questioning what she'd just heard and looking to Larry for confirmation.

"I thought he was a shark," Larry said, as he nodded. "He scared the crap out of me."

"People bump into each other surfing, not floating!" Abbs said, with disbelief on her face. "Let me get this right. You two never met before, and today you bumped into each other out float meditating in the ocean?"

"Yes, and yes," Don said.

"Never met him before," Larry confirmed.

"What are the odds?" Abbs said.

"There are no odds for something like this," Don said.

"Spirit don't miss no tricks, and I don't believe in coincidences. You two met for a reason. And...," She said with emphasis, "You came back with a clue to solving the world peace problem? I'd say this is the beginning of an amazing day. It's nice hearing something positive after all the bombings and people dying yesterday. Everyone's so traumatized. Oh, and speaking of trauma, how's your large Bible bumping friend who was taken away in the ambulance last week? I forgot his name."

"Abe's been in the hospital all week," Don said. "Thanks for asking honey. He finally came out of his coma, so I'd say he's doing a lot better."

"Give thanks for that," Abbs said. "He sure lost a lot of weight recently."

"That's for sure," Don said. "Abe was the biggest loser of our little group. He'd just achieved his hundred-pound weight loss milestone, and then he collapsed on the beach after floating. The doctors haven't figured out why."

"And where's Fonu? He always floats with you."

"Fonu's at home," Don said. "Yesterday's bombings really affected him, and with Abe in the hospital, it was a double whammy for Fonu. You know he has such a big heart."

"Speaking of big hearts," Abbs said with a smile. "Dave came by for a hug earlier. He seems much better lately, and he's talking more too."

"That's good to hear," Don said. "I've been thinking the same thing, but it's hard to be objective when you love someone. After ten years of therapy and three brain surgeries, it finally seems to be helping. Speaking of Dave, we're about to meet him now darling, so we gotta be moving. See you next week."

"I'd love to hear the clue you got to world peace, if you ever want to hang out," Abbs said in a seductive way. "You know, you're the only man I feel comfortable around."

"Okay, I'll tell you," Don said, as he hugged Abbs good-bye, "but I suggest you keep it a secret."

"I promise Don," Abbs said, looking Don in the eyes and crossing her heart slowly, from nipple to nipple.

Don leaned in and whispered in her ear, "Muhammad had a point."

"You mean the Muslim Muhammad?" Abbs asked, in a raised voice.

"Shhh, yes," Don replied, bouncing his hands palms down like he was testing the softness of a pillow. "Yes, the Muslim Muhammad," he whispered.

Abb's face went blank. Don smiled and said, "See you next week darling."

"The Muhammad who dictated the Quran?"

"Yes Abbs," Don replied.

"I really don't know much about Islam except the killings and the bombings," Abbs said, hugging Don goodbye and then hugging Larry. Abbs was shocked. *Why would a good American like Don read the Quran?*

Don and Larry left the shop. Larry grabbed his board and they walked up the hill to the cliffs overlooking Cowell's beach and the wharf. "What got you out floating today?" Larry asked.

"I was letting go of the world peace problem again," Don said. "Yesterday's bombings really affected me. Seeing people cheering, as other people, buried alive, were dying. I couldn't take it. I had to get away from the insanity of the televised world. I just needed to rest my head. It's hard to believe I brought back the idea that Muhammad had a point. It's difficult to admit this to a fellow American. I don't want to be taken out of context."

"Yes, it could sound un-American if taken out of context," Larry said, shaking his head. "Especially after the bombings yesterday, but I get you."

"So... how long have you been floating?" Larry asked.

"Nearly early every week since I was 16. That makes it 12 years," Don replied. "Depending on conditions. If the swell is up, I surf instead. I've been hooked on floating ever since the first time I accidentally tranced out. I'll never forget it. I was right here, and I was way far out over my head. It was a warm calm day like this. I was just floating, trying to breathe slowly without worrying about sinking on the exhale, know what I mean?"

"Yes, I know exactly what you mean," Larry replied. "That's the secret my father taught me, breathing smoothly, without worrying about sinking on the exhale."

"Mind you, I'd never heard of float meditation before," Don said. "It was just another day at the beach, and I was just swimming and floating for fun, like I said, out in deep water over my head. I was just trying to breathe smoothly, when the next thing I knew, I felt sand with my feet and hands. It was like I teleported through time. The feeling of the sand brought me out of my first floating trance. It was a complete accident. It was like I had discovered a new dimension. I was totally jazzed, and I was hooked on floating from then on. Now, when I float, I regularly go out of body and fly through outer space. It helps me solve problems.

"And lately, we've been bringing over a small group from San Jose, but not today," Don said, shaking his head. "With Abe in the hospital and the bombings yesterday, today it's just me and Dave, and Dave doesn't float. We shared a ride over the hill from San Jose early this morning. How about you Larry, what got you out floating today?"

"I've been floating since I was nine," Larry replied. "After my mother died, we moved to Hawaii and I surfed, swam and floated with my father all the time. As I got older, I got into the problem-solving aspects of float meditation. Nowadays I float when I have a big problem, and I need help finding an answer. That's why I'm here today."

"What, traumatized about the bombings yesterday like half the world?" Don asked.

"Of course," Larry replied. "I've been traumatized ever since the first nine-eleven attack. I was about your age then, but that's not the big problem I have today.

"Big problem eh?" Don said with a smile. "That's why I'm here Larry. I love taking on big, seemingly impossible problems."

Don and Larry approached a bench at the top of the hill. "Okay, here we are. This is where Dave and I always meet. Let me hear this big problem you have. I know we bumped into each other for a reason. So, if you have a big problem, I got you man. Let's hear it."

Don was fascinated by this smiling man who was old enough to be his father. Larry Cooley was a good looking, fifty-six-year-old, mixed race, shaven bald American. He was lean and solid with light brown eyes that seemed to shine. He had a deep tan on his reflective head and a big smile full of white teeth.

Don Sanchez was exactly half Larry's age. Don was twenty-eight and still coming to grips with the fact he bumped into this smiling man floating in the ocean. Larry seemed so enlightened and full of spirit, Don thought Larry might be an angel or something.

Don and Larry sat on the bench overlooking the ocean where they had been floating. Don prepared to listen deeply to Larry's big problem, when in the distance, he saw Dave walking back from the lighthouse towards them. "Hold on there Larry," Don said. "Here comes my friend Dave now."

Don stood up and walked over to greet Dave. "Hey brother, how you doing?" Don said, as they greeted each other with a full-on hug. Dave was big, and he nearly lifted Don's five-foot eight-inch lean frame off the ground as they hugged. Dave's smile said it all. He was doing great as usual.

Dave was twenty-eight, the same age as Don to the day. He wore a black patch over his left eye that made him look like a big mean pirate, but Dave wasn't mean. He was nice. Dave was a nice, very strong and fit, six-foot three-inch man with a black eye patch. He had dirty blond hair down just passed his neck, tan skin, clean white teeth and gums that were nicely pink. Dave had some brain damage, but other than that, he still shined with his huge smile and his bright green right eye the color of a Redwood tree.

"Larry, I'd like you to meet my long-time best friend Dave Hetfield. Dave, I'd like you to meet my new friend Larry."

Larry and Dave shook hands as Don tried to remember Larry's last name, "Let's see, your name was very cool. That's it! Cooley! Larry Cooley. You won't believe it Dave! Larry and I were both tranced out floating and we literally bumped into each other out there. What do you think of that?"

Say what? Dave had a questioning look on his face. He wrinkled his forehead. He was thinking hard about what he had just heard.

Don repeated, "Yes, Dave. You heard me right. We were both tranced out float meditating, and we literally bumped into each other. Can you believe that?"

"Wow," Dave said softly. Dave understood the incredible odds of such an event.

"Dave doesn't talk a lot nowadays," Don said, "and when he does, he talks a little slow. He had a bad accident ten years ago, and it really affected his talkativeness, but he hears and understands everything just fine. See that eye patch? Doesn't it make him look like a pirate?" Don said, winking at Larry with a big smile on his face.

Larry got the hint. "Yes, Dave does look like a pirate," Larry said, as Dave smiled.

"The accident gave him some brain damage. Essentially, it gave him a frontal lobotomy."

"Par-tial!" Dave said in a raised voice, separating the syllables and stomping his foot, while looking at Don with his one good eye.

"Sorry Dave," Don said. "Actually Larry, the accident gave Dave a partial frontal lobotomy, and Dave gets upset when I leave out the partial part."

"Understandably so, that would bother me too," Larry said. "Life's hard enough without getting partially lobotomized."

Dave smiled hearing this. "It's Okay," Dave said softly, moving his palms up to the sky like it was no big deal.

"Larry has a big problem and we're going to help him," Don said. "What do you think about that Dave?" Dave smiled and put his two thumbs up to the sky.

"That's great Dave," Don said. "But you need to use your voice if you want your brain to get better."

"Sounds good Don," Dave said slowly.

"How about I give you guys a ride back to San Jose?" Larry asked. "My rig and my problem are only two blocks away."

"Your rig?" Don replied. "So, it's not a car. What do you think Dave? Shall we hitch a ride with Larry?" Dave put his thumbs up to the sky, as Don just looked at him and waited.

"Sorry Don. Yes, Larry seems cool," Dave said slowly.

Larry picked up his board and started walking. Don was right beside him and Dave was close behind. Dave didn't say a word as they walked, but he listened to everything. Dave heard every word.

CHAPTER 9

Larry's Good Idea

"Here's my rig now," Larry said, as he loaded his board on the gigantic vehicle.

"What the hell is this?" Don asked, with an amazed look on his face. "A fire truck from outer space?" Don stroked his dark brown beard as he walked around the huge vehicle.

"She's my own personal rescue vehicle," Larry said. "Isn't she beautiful? Her name's Alice. So now, do you think I'm crazy or what?"

"I'll choose or what, until I understand the whole story," Don replied.

"Thanks Don. All I can say is, it sounded like a good idea at the time, so I did it."

"This rig is out of this world. What do you think Dave?" Don asked as he walked around the amazing vehicle. Don's dark brown eyes were wide open. His mouth was open too, as he ran his fingers through his thick dark brown hair. Then a big smile formed on his face. Don was blown away.

Larry's rescue rig was huge. It was a fuel cell powered customized Tesla Semi that looked like a cross between a gigantic tow truck and a fire truck equipped for all sorts of rescues. It had a telescoping lift that could go up five stories with outriggers for stability, and a fire hose on a turret, and it carried a thousand-gallon tank of water. It had a jaws-of-life, a forty-ton electric winch and several portable respirators. It had a tool rack with chain saws, pry bars, saws-all's and axes. Larry's rig was equipped with everything one might need in an emergency.

"This looks like the ultimate rolling rescue rig," Don said.

"Yes she is," Larry said, "with a fully outfitted sleeper, micro kitchen and shower."

"You've got everything here Larry! Have you actually rescued people?" Don asked.

"Yes, I have," Larry replied. "Thank God for that. If not, I'd sure look like an idiot right now. Those first couple years were difficult, until I had my first rescue. You know, people can be brutal."

"Bullies pick on the one who stands out," Don said. "And you sure as hell stand out driving this thing around."

"It helped me learn not to care what people think," Larry said. "That's when I found some peace."

"People sure are strange," Don said. "So, what's your big problem? She looks brand new and in excellent shape."

"No problems with Alice here," Larry replied. "She's in top notch shape. My problem's inside."

CHAPTER 10

Damsel in Distress

"Don, Dave. There's someone inside I'd like you to meet. She doesn't speak. She only nods her head or shakes it, and she shook it like crazy when I suggested calling the authorities. She hasn't spoken a word since I rescued her. Or, I don't know, maybe I'm aiding and abetting her. This is my big problem, and I sure could use some help."

Larry opened the door, and softly said, "I don't know your name yet, but these are my new friends Don and Dave. They're very friendly, and I promise you'll be safe. We're going to help you. Don take shotgun. Dave, hop in the back. Let's go to San Jose."

Don and Dave climbed in. Don immediately turned around with his big smile and a look that made people feel comfortable and warm inside. Don had a look that made people feel like everything was going to be okay. "Hi, I'm Don and this is my oldest friend Dave," Don said, as he reached out and offered his hand to the girl. "Nice to meet you. Dave looks like a big pirate, doesn't he? He's actually very nice."

The girl shook Don's hand politely, as Dave smiled at Don's pirate comment. Then she extended her hand to Dave and said, "My name's Don too. I'm Donna, but my friends call me Don."

"She speaks!" Larry exclaimed. "Give thanks for that. One problem solved."

Donna was a very pretty, petite girl. She looked extremely fit, like a runner, with dyed blond hair having very dark roots that set off the single ivy vine tattoo creeping up her neck. She had lots of piercings all over her head and nice little tea-cup breasts. She wasn't wearing a bra and her nipples were clearly outlined through the thin fabric of her long-sleeved white shirt. She had piercings in her eyebrows, ears and lips, but most obvious was the large dark septum ring hanging off her nose. That nose ring really stood out, but she was so pretty, it didn't matter. Donna was beautiful, and Don and Dave were immediately attracted to her.

"Yes, I speak," Donna said. "I was just scared and all alone, and I didn't know if I could trust you. I didn't talk because I didn't know if you were a nut or what, driving this thing around, listening to emergency radio calls, talking about God and your big purpose in life. I thought maybe you were a wacko."

"That's understandable," Don said with a big smile, as Dave giggled a little.

"But no problem enter the large blonde pirate and smiling mystic man. Anyway, at least you're talking and seem comfortable now. I'm very grateful for that," Larry said, as he rolled his eyes and added, "I get no respect."

"I want to thank you for rescuing me Larry," Donna said. "I was in such distress, but now I feel safe."

"You actually do rescue people!" Don exclaimed. "I love it. Wait, did she just say what I think she said?"

Dave was nodding. He heard it too. "Larry rescued a damsel in distress," Dave said slowly, with a big smile on his face.

"That's what I do," Larry said. "Ready to go to San Jo?"

"Sounds good to me," Don said. "Where do you live Donna?"

"San Jose is as good as any place," Donna replied.

"Are you homeless?" Don asked.

"I'm just really tired," Donna said, as she laid back her head and shut her eyes.

"Let her sleep," Larry said. "I think she's been up and on the run for a couple days."

"Okay, let's go," Don said.

CHAPTER II

Know It All's Who Don't Know it All

Larry put his rig in gear and pulled out. "So, tell me about you and Dave," Larry said. "You seem close, like brothers or something."

"Hear that Dave?" Don asked, looking back. Dave was smiling and nodding his head.

"It's a long story, where should I start?" Don asked.

"Beginning," Dave answered from the back seat.

"Okay, in the beginning Dave lived in the Santa Cruz Mountains in a house surrounded by redwood trees, and Dave loves redwood trees don't you Dave?"

"Yup," Dave said, smiling.

"Well, it was during a terrible storm, in the middle of the night, while everyone was sleeping," Don said, getting a little emotional. "One of the biggest redwood trees fell. It crashed through the roof killing both his parents and his twin sisters instantly. Only Dave survived."

"Oh, I'm so sorry Dave," Larry said.

"It's okay," Dave said, putting his palms up.

Donna didn't respond, except for a tear rolling down here cheek. She was pretending to be asleep, but she was listening to everything.

"Dave ended up with a foster family in the house next door to mine, so we became best friends," Don said, trying to be positive. "And then it gets worse again."

"What? Dave's whole family got killed, and it gets worse?" Larry asked.

"Yes, but there were lots of good times too, weren't there Dave?" Dave smiled and nodded.

"Dave and I rode our bicycles everywhere around San Jose and the whole South San Francisco Bay Area. Everywhere we went Dave took pictures of trees, and he worked hard to learn their names. He knew most by their Latin names too, huh Dave." Dave smiled and nodded again.

"We spent a lot of time with my father building hot rods and robots back then too. We had a big garage out back with a full machine shop, small clean room and a bad ass electronics lab. My father taught us all about electronics and fixing up old hot rods, including machining all the parts. We build some hot rods with Dad, didn't we Dave?"

"And robots," Dave said from the back.

"You know life's a mixture of good and bad and normal and strange. Well, Dave's foster parents were strange, and their house was very cluttered with lots of small tables and bookshelves full of breakable things. And there were four other foster kids running around, so things got broken often. And when something got broken, pure madness came out of

Dave's foster mother. She would scream and yell and invent all kinds of punishments for the kids. Dave stayed away as much as possible. He spent most of the time over at my house. Now he's like my brother.

"There definitely were a lot of good times," Don said. "Then came the day of Dave's accident, and once again, it was a tree that changed the course of Dave's life. Dave loved trees so much. He loved riding his bike under the limbs with his hands up in the air, like he was surfing in a tube or something. He loved standing on his pedals and brushing his hair against the leaves. Dave loved riding under the trees.

"Well, on that fateful day, there was a freshly pruned prune tree with very sharp tips on its freshly pruned branches, *Prunus* in Latin isn't it Dave?"

"*Prunus serrulata*," Dave said slowly. "The Japanese flowering cherry."

Don continued, "It was dusk, and the light was fading. Dave was riding, standing up on his pedals, like he always did. He was coasting, about to brush his hair against the leaves, when suddenly, he got a sharp branch through his left eye socket and into the frontal lobe of his brain."

"Ouch," Larry grimaced, "Yes, you told me about his accident."

"Sorry for the gory details, but Dave's lobotomy is a big part of a much bigger story."

"Partial!" Dave exclaimed, slapping the back of Don's seat. He was embarrassed having Donna hear about his brain damage.

"Yes, of course Dave, my bad," Don said.

"Gosh, life's hard enough without losing your family and getting partially lobotomized," Larry said. "You seem to be doing great Dave."

"It's okay," Dave said.

"That was ten years ago," Don said. "He's doing much better now, give thanks for that, but after the accident Dave was bad. He was in a deep coma for two months. We didn't know if he was going to wake up or die or be a vegetable or normal or what. Then, after he woke up, he was in the hospital for another two months.

"School was over for the summer, so I visited Dave every day. I prayed and asked God why, but I got no reply. Then I saw his foster parent's reaction, and it made me sick to my stomach. It was the furthest thing from love I could imagine. It was pure selfishness. It was evil. And it was then, I knew evil existed. They gave up on Dave exactly when he needed help most.

"You see, Dave turned eighteen in the hospital. So, legally, his foster parents were off the hook. They called the authorities, relinquished their responsibilities, and walked out on him. When his foster father told me, he actually seemed happy. He said Dave was not his problem or responsibility anymore. He smirked, and it was then, I felt his coldness. It was then, I could see evil in his eyes.

"At the time, it sounded like a really good idea for me to take care of Dave. So, I brought him home and set him up in my bed. Then I told my parents, but they thought I was crazy, because Dave was really effed up, weren't you Dave?"

"Yup," Dave said, smiling and nodding his head.

"My parents didn't get it," Don said. "They didn't understand. They thought I volunteered to sacrifice their freedom and happiness. They didn't think I could take care of Dave on my own, and they made it clear, they weren't going to be Dave's caregivers.

"My parents were angry because I brought Dave home without talking with them first. You know, communication is so important. They definitely were not happy about it, but at the end of the day, they agreed to let Dave stay temporarily until I found a place and moved out. I took Dave under my wing and did the paperwork to become his legal guardian. That was ten years ago, and today here we are, and Dave's a whole lot better."

"Hey Don, did you say it sounded like a good idea at the time?" Larry asked.

"I said, 'At the time it sounded like a really good idea,' but it's the same thing."

"That's exactly what I thought when I decided to spend three million on this rescue rig," Larry said. "It sounded like a good idea at the time. A truly good idea, like your idea to help Dave, all good, nothing bad or selfish, just pure good, pure love."

"Pure love, deciding to buy a gigantic pimped-out rescue-mobile? What do you mean Larry?" Don asked, although he knew the answer. Don knew the importance of truly good ideas, but he wanted to hear it from Larry.

"These truly good ideas we have are formed with God, even if they seem a little crazy at the time," Larry said. "Like your idea to take care of Dave seemed a little crazy to your parents, but I see the pure good. You know we live in a sea of selfishness."

"You think your good idea to spend millions on this rescue rig was some kind of good idea from God?" Don asked.

"Yes, just like your good idea to take care of Dave. Don't you see? You rescued Dave."

"Okay, I guess, but most people are going to think you're nuts if you go around saying your great idea came from God. You saw how Donna reacted. Most people don't get it, but not me Larry. I'm with you on the good ideas at the time thing, especially now I know you rescued four people."

"Thanks Don."

"No worries man. Now, where were we? Oh yes, Dave's foster parents. They were of the super Christian variety, weren't they Dave?"

Dave nodded, then he shook his head slowly with his palms up like, what are you going to do?

"They were well trained Christian fundamentalists who had a problem communicating about anything new," Don said. "According to Dave's foster father, everyone was going to hell unless they believed exactly like him. Look, I enjoy discussing theology, especially the problems with big organized religions, but with him it got old fast. I noticed there was nothing getting in. It was like he wasn't listening. It reminded me of debating with the communists at Berkeley. In the end, he became more like a tape recorder than a thinking person. He just pointed his stubby finger at me and screamed, 'Everyone needs a moral authority! Either you believe the Bible is God's inerrant word, or not. Yes or no! That's all I need to know about you and where you're going!'

"I told him I believed the Bible was valuable to read, and I thought it contained great wisdom, but absolutely perfect, every word, every verse, translated by humans, interpreted by men? Why did every word have to be perfect? And why did his interpretation have to be perfect too? I told him that insisting his own interpretation was perfect was conceited. Needless to say, Dave's foster father didn't like me very much. He called me Satan's offspring."

"He didn't like any of my friends," Dave said slowly.

"We're all imperfect," Larry said. "It's one of the Bible's main themes. It sounds like he was a know-it-all-who-didn't-know-it-all."

"That's for sure," Don said. "He couldn't admit the possibility he might be one percent wrong about anything. All I knew was, he walked out on Dave right when Dave needed help most and that was bad. I loved Dave. So, I was all in.

"Our friend Fonu Ali agreed to help Dave too. Fonu put in money he received from Saudi Arabia as compensation for the death of his father in the Hajj. I sold a race car I won in a robotics contest at the university, and we combined our resources for a down payment on an old Victorian fixer upper near the bus stop. Then we all moved in and got to work.

"Fonu worked on the house, while I telecommuted and did most of the caring for Dave. We needed big money for Dave's brain surgery, and we had lots of bills to pay, so we both thought up ways to bring in more money. Fonu's first brainstorm was burying two forty by eight-foot cargo containers in the back yard. He converted them into living spaces we rent out to illegal immigrants and young artists."

"What?" Larry asked. "Are you serious Don? You have artists and illegal immigrants living out back, underground, in cargo containers?"

"Who could afford to live normally in San Jose?" Don replied. "Think of it as six micro-hotels, we rent out to help cover expenses." Don saw the expression on Larry's face. "Look, in the beginning taking care of Dave was a full-time job. We needed money coming in fast, because Dave needed brain surgery really bad. You know, the government insurance doesn't cover much.

"Dave's had three brain surgeries so far, and he has another one coming up in Mexico in two weeks. He'll be bald again just like you Larry. Okay, our exit is coming up. Take the Alameda exit and turn right. Okay, now get in the left lane. We'll be turning left up ahead."

Larry stopped at the light, as Don continued talking, "Yes, they each have their own clean, safe place with electricity. And they all share a nice, clean, shower and bathroom facility. They have everything they need, but most of all they help pay the mortgage."

"You won a robotics contest?" Larry asked.

"Yes, I have a knack for mechanics and mathematics," Don said. "It helps having professors for parents. The software was the key to winning. I built a beautiful mechanical hand and came up with some algorithms that used artificial intelligence to let my hand help create its own software. The skin had pressure sensors throughout to control the gripping force. It worked perfectly as planned. At the end of the day, all the sponsors wanted was the software. And I won an expensive race car."

"And you sold it to help Dave," Larry said. "You really are brothers."

"Okay, slow down, see that lady walking, she's right in front of our house."

"Nice old Victorian," Larry said.

"There's Fonu on the porch with his guitar watching us roll up in the coolest ride in town."

"Thanks Don."

"From one mechanical dude to another, I like this ride. Pull in the driveway and you can park right there," Don said, pointing to the driveway between his and his neighbor's house.

"I'll be pretty close," Larry said. "Are you sure your neighbor won't mind?"

"Yes, it'll be a little tight," Don said. "But I'm sure we can work something out. All it takes is communication. There's Gerry now. Gerry's my very friendly, and very flamboyant, gay psychiatrist neighbor. I'm sure he'll throw a tizzy fit, but not to worry. Oh, and here comes Fonu too. This should be fun." Don had a big smile on his face. He turned to Donna and said, "Donna, one word of caution about Fonu. Donna are you awake?"

Donna was pretending to be asleep, but she was listening to everything. Now, she was stretching her petite torso with her hands clenched up in the air. "Yes, I'm awake."

"I need to warn you about Fonu's mouth," Don said, looking at Donna seriously. "Once you get to know him, I know you'll love him, but Fonu has a problem with his mouth. I don't know what it is exactly, but I think it's a strange variation of Tourette's syndrome. He just blurts out whatever's on his mind at the time without a politically correct filter, or filter of any kind. He says things that, taken the wrong way, might seem offensive. But trust me, underneath it all, Fonu has a heart of gold. I'm sure he'll want to know about your tattoos and piercings. He'll want to know their deep meaning." Don was mainly thinking about the big dark ring hanging right down in the middle of her nose. "Just be prepared, because Fonu Ali will definitely say something. He always does, just be ready for it."

"Okay, I guess," Donna said, with a puzzled look on her face.

CHAPTER 12

Sounded Like a Good Idea at the Time

Larry parked his gigantic rig exactly where Don had pointed. Don's neighbor Gerry came running over waving his hands in the air exclaiming, "My word this thing is so biiiiigg." Gerry pronounced the 'i' in the word big like in the word bee. "It's so biiiiigg," Gerry repeated, putting his fingers to his lips briefly. "This thing is huge. It's absolutely gi-normous."

"Hello Gerry. How are you?" Don asked through the open window of the cab.

Gerry grabbed the hand hold, hopped up on the step, and lisped, "I'm feeling abtholutely wonderful today Don, thank you, and you? You're looking handsome as ever. Oh, hi Dave. I see you back there. You're looking piratey as ever. My word, you have a girl in there," Gerry said, putting his fingers to his lips again.

Gerry was a fifty-three-year-old, five-foot seven-inch, part Chinese, part African American. He was very lean, wore a goatee and had very short, dark, kinky hair. He was one third bald and one hundred percent flamboyant homosexual.

Fonu Ali came walking over as Don, Dave, Larry and Donna climbed down from the cab. Fonu Ali was big, large boned, fat and hairy. He pushed the scales past three-fifty. He was Tongan on his mother's side, and Afghani on his father's. His sturdy bones came from his mother. His hairiness came from his father. His fatness came from eating too much, and he knew it. Fonu Ali was very sensitive about his weight."

Fonu looked very Tongan due to his large size and afro hair style, but his hairiness made him distinctly different than most Tongan men, who are not very hairy. Fonu Ali was very big and very hairy. "What's this thing you're riding in Don, and who are they?" Fonu Ali asked.

"Hello Fonu, this thing is just your size, don't you think?" Gerry asked, with a slightly evil grin.

"Don't get me going Gerry," Fonu Ali said. "The bombings yesterday really affected me. They're still digging people out! Do you realize that? People are suffering right now and could be taking their last breath. I'm traumatized, and I'm not in the mood for your big mouth."

"Traumatized? Oh Fonu, my poor baby. Just let it out, let it out. You can tell me anything. You can always come over and lie down on my couch," Gerry said, batting his eyes at Fonu.

"Shut up Gerry," Fonu said, with a scowl on his face.

"You two just be nice," Don said. "Gerry Long and Fonu Ali, I'd like you to meet Donna and Larry."

"Why hello there Larry. My you have a big rig. It's so huge. It's so very nice to meet you," Gerry said, extending his hand, palm down, fingers forward, like a debutante at a grand ball. "I'm Gerry, Don's gay psychiatrist neighbor."

Larry attempted to shake Gerry's hand normally, but he could only grab his fingertips. It was a very awkward handshake to say the least. "Nice to meet you too," Larry said politely, as Gerry curtsied.

"What's this huuuuge thing you're driving around Larry?" Gerry asked in a deep voice. Then his voice shifted to the opposite extreme, "It sure is biiiggg!" He wined.

"It's my own personal rescue vehicle," Larry said.

"Obviously, but I've never heard of anyone driving around in their own personal rescue vehicle before," Gerry said.

"Are you sure you're not a nutcase?" Fonu asked.

"I think the jury's out on that question," Larry replied.

"Good answer, at least you're honest. I'm Fonu Ali."

"You most thertainly are," Gerry lisped.

"I wasn't talking to you Gerry," Fonu said, scrunching his eyebrows and giving Gerry a mean stare.

"Did I say I was a psychiatrist?" Gerry asked. "I'm a medical doctor you know. I can help. Have you ever heard of the superhero disorder? I think this is a classic case."

"He's not crazy Gerry," Don said. "He said it sounded like good idea at the time. And since then, he's saved four people's lives."

"Did you say it sounded like a good idea at the time?" Gerry asked, putting a finger to his lips again and looking at Don.

"Yes, I did Gerry," Don said, in a slightly raised voice, with his eyes wide open looking at Gerry.

"Those were my exact words," Larry interjected. "It sounded like a good idea at the time."

"My word! You've got to be kidding me?" Gerry asked.

"No, I'm not kidding you Gerry," Don said, still looking at Gerry.

"We were just talking about good ideas the other day," Gerry said. "You said that's how you think God talks to us, even me, through our truly good ideas. Oh, I think I'm going to cry. Maybe God does love me. Maybe God is out there, trying to help me by giving me good ideas? Either that or it's just a big coincidence."

"Like bumping into someone float meditating in the ocean is just a big coincidence?" Don said.

"My word, that would be a biiiiig coincidence," Gerry squealed.

"Exactly," Don said. "Today in the ocean with Larry."

"You mean that actually happened?" Gerry asked, questioning what he'd just heard. "You both thought it sounded like a good idea to go floating? And then you bumped into each other out float meditating in the ocean?"

"Yes Gerry," Don replied, looking at Gerry. Like, do you finally get it?

"I think I believe in God again," Gerry said. "And I believe Don is the best shrink on the block."

"Give me a break!" Fonu Ali exclaimed. "You're just kissing Don's ass. Last week you were a rabid atheist, and what, now you believe in miracles? I don't believe it."

"Lighten up Fonu," Don said. "Gerry's been traumatized by the church, like a lot of us. He'll argue against anything that sounds even the least bit religious. People say they don't believe, but mostly they've just had it with the insanity and politics of the super religious. In that regard, he's really just like us."

"Gerry's not anything like us," Fonu grumbled, with a sour look on his face.

"It's beer o'clock," Dave said.

"That it is," Don said smiling, with his eyes open wide and all his teeth showing.

"Sounds like you're making progress Gerry. See you tomorrow."

"Now wait Don, wait, wait just a minute," Gerry said. "What about Larry's gigantic rig parked in front of my roses and my kitchen window? I'm so sorry. I'm so so, oh so, sorry Larry. You just can't park this huge thing here. It's tooooo biiiiigggg. It's out of the question. I won't be able to see you guys singing on the porch, and my roses won't get any sun."

"Oh, come on now Gerry. It's not going to kill you or your roses," Don said.

"Ooooh Dooon, you know I only want to please you," Gerry moaned, with a finger to his lips. Gerry was thinking really hard. "I think I have a really good idea. It's not world peace, but it's a start. Larry can park his big rig in front of my roses, if I can come over for beers at five O'clock."

"No. Absolutely not. Anything but that," Fonu Ali said.

"Anything?" Gerry said, batting his eyes at Fonu.

"Look Fonu," Don said. "There's no other place for Larry to park nearby, and all Gerry wants is to come over for a beer. That sounds perfectly reasonable to me. What do you think Dave?"

Dave gave the thumbs up sign, as Don just waited, looking at Dave until he said something. "Sounds good Don," Dave said slowly.

"Of course, we can have Gerry over for a beer or two," Don said. "It's not going to kill you Fonu."

"Or two? Oohh," Fonu sighed, closing his eyes and shaking his head slowly.

Gerry immediately got a big smile on his face and began bouncing his fingertips together saying, "Goody, goody gumdrops we're going to have some fun. We're going to have some fun."

Fonu just grunted, frowned and pushed his lips out. Fonu Ali pushes his lips out on the rare occasions he has nothing to say.

"You two just get along," Don said. "That's what it's all about."

Fonu was quiet with his lips still pushed out.

"Thank you, Don," Gerry said. "I'll slip into something more comfortable and be right over."

"Something more comfortable? What the hell's he going to wear? Furry slippers and a tutu?" Fonu wined.

"Who am I to judge?" Don said, shrugging his shoulders and putting his palms up to the sky.

As Gerry was changing, everyone else walked up to the house. "Hello Donna, nice to meet you," Fonu Ali said, as he offered his large hand to the petite, pierced and tattooed girl.

"Nice to meet you too," Donna said, as they shook hands. "You can call me Don."

"I think that would be too confusing," Fonu said.

"Okay, call me Donna then."

"Why do you have a single ivy vine tattooed up your neck?" Fonu asked. "What does it mean? Do you feel suffocated?"

"It's body art," Donna replied. "It doesn't have to mean anything."

"Meaningless art?" Fonu queried, with his forehead all scrunched up.

Oh, here it comes. This is what Don warned me about. "Never mind Fonu. Don warned me about your mouth and I'm not playing."

"What's your problem?" Fonu asked. "You sure have an attitude."

"I've been through a lot," Donna replied.

"Haven't we all? What about all those piercings, don't they get infected sometimes?" Fonu asked.

"Sometimes, at first," she replied. *What's with this interrogation?*

"What about that big dark ring hanging off your nose?" Fonu asked.

"What about it?" Donna replied assertively.

"Does it signify something?"

"What?" Donna replied defiantly. Now, she was staring at Fonu directly and very aware of the ring dangling off her nose.

"I think they pierced it too close to the end of your nose," Fonu said. "Either that or it's just too big or too dark. I can't help but stare at it when I'm talking to you. Why would a pretty girl like you wear a bull ring in her nose? It's smaller, but it's similar to a ring a bull would have in its nose. It only detracts from your looks. So, I was just wondering, does it signify something?"

"I can't take this crap! I'm so out of here!" Donna exclaimed, as she stormed away and ran down the street.

"You did it again Fonu, didn't you?" Don said, shaking his head. "You and your big mouth."

"I'm sorry Don. I didn't mean to," Fonu Ali said.

"I know. You never mean to. You just blurt out whatever's on your mind, and people get their feelings hurt," Don said, as he ran out after Donna. Fonu followed, walking slowly with his head down like a bad dog.

Don caught up with Donna and said, "I'm sorry Donna. I don't know what Fonu said that upset you, but let's stop and talk about it for a minute, rather than give up."

"I don't know Don. Sometimes, I think my purpose is to be alone, away from other people."

"I feel you, but I can guarantee that's not true," Don said. "Humans say the wrong things sometimes, but I'm happy you're still talking with me."

"Oh Don, you're great!" Donna said. "But I don't see why you live with Fonu. He's obviously homophobic, and you were right about his mouth."

"First of all, you barely even know me. So, don't say I'm great. You have no idea the plans I have going on up here. I know you can't read my mind," Don said, pointing to his head. "There are lots of bad people out there."

"I wasn't asleep on the drive," Donna said. "I heard everything about how you've been helping Dave. I heard how you sold your prized car, and how you buried bunkers in your backyard. I heard everything, and I think that's radical love."

"But Donna, you need to understand, Fonu's been as much a part of helping Dave as I have. And don't forget, he has a syndrome. It's like a twitch that comes out of his mouth. He says the strangest things, and it's always exactly what he's thinking. It's rarely anything all that bad. Can you please just give Fonu another chance?" Don said, putting his right arm across Donna's shoulders giving her a one arm hug. "Actually, I think this might be good for him. Maybe it'll shake him up a little. He needs to learn to think before he speaks, like a lot of people. So, tell me, what was it he said that upset you?"

"He asked about my septum ring. He called it a bull ring and said it was pierced too close to the end of my nose. And that it was too big and dark, and that it was the only thing he could think about while he was talking with me."

"Oh," Don said, touching his chin and stretching his mouth uncomfortably.

"He asked me if it signified something."

"Well, we guys can't understand why beautiful girls like you wear them," Don said. "Most of us are too polite to ask, but not Fonu. In a way, I think it's his gift. A gift, that's sometimes a curse."

"It's none of his freeking business!" Donna exclaimed.

"I agree," Don said. "But you need to understand, Fonu's an artist. He sees your tattoos and piercings from an artist's point of view. He sees you, like he is, an artist screaming to be noticed. An artist saying please understand my work! Fonu sees, and Fonu speaks exactly what's on his mind, that's all. One thing about Fonu, he's honest, and it's his honesty that gets him in trouble.

"Regarding Fonu's problem with Gerry, I must confess, Fonu and I are both recovering homophobes. Fonu was reared by a homophobic Muslim father. I just had a bad experience. Either way, people can become homophobic. Fonu's words convict him. I just have to deal with the thoughts in my head.

"At least Fonu and I admit it, and we're working on it. Hell, we're just about to have a beer with our flaming gay psychiatrist neighbor. You wouldn't want to miss that, would you? Here comes Fonu now. Look at him. He's upset. Go give him a hug honey. Everything's going to be okay. He has a loose tongue, but he has a heart of gold. Be certain Donna, you're in a safe place here."

"Thanks for explaining things Don," she said, as she walked towards Fonu.

"Oh Donna, I'm sorry," Fonu said, with his arms open wide, and his big eyes wet with tears. Fonu was radiating love at that moment and Donna could feel it. She went to him and received a big Fonu bear hug.

"My mouth gets me in trouble all the time," Fonu said.

"I was warned," Donna replied. "I guess you have some kind of syndrome or something?"

"Yeh, I just blurt out whatever I'm thinking. Don thinks it's a special gift because it starts conversations. And you're such a beautiful girl, I just can't understand why you would…" Fonu paused.

"What? Make myself less beautiful?" Donna said.

"Yes," Fonu replied.

"If you got as much unwanted attention as I do, you might do something about it too," she said.

"That's a problem I don't have," Fonu said.

"Come on you two," Don said. "Let's grab a beer."

"Sounds good to me," Fonu said, as they walked back to the house.

Dave greeted Donna at the door. "Everything okay?" Dave asked slowly, in a caring way.

"We're all good Dave. Thanks for asking," Donna replied, and then she gave Dave a big hug.

CHAPTER 13

Welcome to Group Therapy

They went into the house, through a foyer, and into a very large room. It had wood floors and wood walls and many plants hanging from the ceiling. There were wandering jews, spider plants and ferns slowly turning near the open windows. The artwork on the walls was all original and strategically placed. It was a very cool space.

There wasn't much furniture. It was really bare bones, except for all the plants and eight large comfy chairs, arranged like a circle of thrones, in the center of the room. Donna was taking in all the paintings, which were beautiful, unique, abstract and realistic. She checked out the comfy chairs and picked the big green velvet one, kicked off her shoes and settled in. "Did you paint all these Fonu?" Donna asked. "I really like them."

"Yes I paint a lot," Fonu said. "Thank you."

At that moment, Gerry Long came floating into the room. He twirled a white boa and wore a rainbow chiffon jumpsuit that was partially see through. "Beer me please," he said, as he strutted with his fingers out, palms to the floor, like a model on a runway, moving his arms back and forth."

Fonu Ali looked at Don and shook his head, "I'm just sending telepathy," Fonu said.

"What's that you're wearing Gerry?" Don asked. "Your gay pride outfit?"

"It's just a little something I slipped on Don. Do you like it?" Gerry asked, as he did a spin, holding the boa up with one hand.

"No, not exactly Gerry. I can't say I do," Don replied, visibly agitated. "That thing looks like a negligee! It's freeking see through. Shoot man! We're regular dudes! You come over for a beer with us dressed like that? What are we supposed to think? This is a beer with the boys not some perverted crap."

"I can tell you're a little uncomfortable," Gerry said.

"That's like saying I'm a little fat," Fonu Ali said, with his eyebrows all scrunched together.

"Look Gerry," Don said very compassionately. "I shared with you that Fonu and I had our homophobic awakenings. We both awoke to the fact we were indeed homophobic and needed to change. I also shared that we were still working on it, and we weren't one hundred percent there yet. How do you think we feel seeing you dressed in that? For a second, put the shoe on the other foot okay? Can you tell I'm a little off my cool?"

"Yes Don. I'm terribly sorry," Gerry said, putting a finger to his lips. "I'm so sorry I made you feel uncomfortable."

"Actually Gerry, in that outfit, you're the perfect illustration of the gay activist extreme we need to communicate with.

You see, we're trying hard to be gay friendly and gay accepting, but at the same time, we disagree with the gay activist extreme, which you represent prancing around in a see-through wisp of a garment like that. You see, being gay friendly is one thing, but feeling forced to accept the activist extreme is another."

"It's all part of our theory," Fonu said.

"My word Don, I'm so sorry," Gerry said. "For a moment there I thought you were getting angry, and I didn't think you ever got angry."

"I rarely do," Don said. "I only get angry at the insanity man. Like when gay activists drive people away from gay acceptance and religious extremists drive people away from the supernatural. It's crazy! Now, seeing you dressed like that," Don laughed, "I'm feeling it."

"Now, I feel so stupid in this thing," Gerry said. "I'm so sorry Fonu, will you ever forgive me?"

"Hey Don, I forgot," Fonu Ali said. "Why was it we were trying to be gay friendly again?"

"World peace man, that's what it's all about," Don said. "Gotta love your neighbor man."

"And love your enemy," Fonu Ali said, curling up his lip at Gerry.

"Right now, we're working on loving our neighbor," Don said. "And Gerry that's you. We're trying to love you by inviting you over for a beer. How are you loving your neighbor Gerry?"

"That's us," Fonu said defiantly. "You didn't even shave your legs. And what's that you're wearing underneath, a G-string?"

"Thorry Fonu, you don't get to thee," Gerry lisped. "Oh, I see Don. You think I'm trying to seduce you guys and turn you all gay, so we can play train or something? Oh no Don, by all means no. Now I feel so silly. Let me go home and man up a bit. I'll put on some jeans and a tee-shirt. Then can I come back? Please Don?"

"Of course, Gerry," Don said, giggling a little about the crazy world he was living in. Gerry Long ran out, his rainbow chiffon flowing, his white boa trailing in the breeze.

"A black Chinese man with a goatee in a rainbow chiffon jumpsuit and white boa," Larry said, with a big smile. "Gotta love it."

Gerry was back in five minutes dressed like one of the guys, except his jeans were much tighter, and his tee shirt was bright pink, and he was walking funny. He was walking in long strides like a cowboy wearing a gun belt or something. He tucked his thumbs in his waistband, and said, "I'm back men. What do you think?" Gerry said, once again the center of attention.

"Much better," Don said. "Now, can we have a normal conversation without the side show."

"And without thinking you want to poke us in the ass," Fonu said.

"Fonu, Fonu, Fonu, is that what you think?" Gerry asked.

"Well, you're such a flamer," Fonu said, now slightly embarrassed. "And it's like every word that comes out of your mouth has two different meanings, and one is always sexual."

"Do you mean thexual double entendre Fonu?" Gerry lisped. "The thexual part comes from your own brain you know."

"Don't put it all back on me Gerry!" Fonu exclaimed with a scowl. "You need to own your words and how you were dressed earlier!"

"Yes, I know Fonu. I'm sooo bad, especially with my mouth like you." And then Gerry pushed his lips out and erotically moaned, "My mouth is ooh, soo bad."

"That's exactly what I'm talking about!" Fonu exclaimed. "Don! Gerry said he was going to man up, but he's not."

"Oh Fonu, I'm sorry," Gerry said. "You're just so fun to tease. But seriously, I would never try to change your sexual orientation. Listen, I tried to change mine, that's for sure. I was taught that being gay was an evil choice people made, and I lived with that tape running through my head for a long time. It almost drove me crazy. I asked God to make me straight. I prayed with all my heart, like my life depended on it, but it didn't work.

"Then, when I was seventeen, I came out to all my friends at church. They laid their hands on me and prayed, but that didn't work either. I still couldn't stop thinking about penises and large, bearded men. Soon after that, the people at church stopped talking to me. I was totally shunned, and I lost all my church friends."

"Church friends?" Larry asked.

"Yes, if you can believe it, my parents were Bible believing evangelical Christians. Therefore, that's what I was," Gerry said, putting a finger to his lips again. Then he crossed his heart and said, "God's truth. I was as active as a high schooler could be, in the church that is. I was a cheerleader too, but I was the one who needed cheering up inside. I was struggling to make sense of what the church leaders were saying, as well as what was going on in my heart and in my pants."

"What were they saying?" Larry asked.

"That God doesn't make people gay," Gerry replied assertively. "That God doesn't make mistakes. That gay people choose sin like a heroin addict chooses drugs. That it's impossible for two people of the same sex to be in love. All I knew was, I was." Gerry put his hands together and swooned to the side. "I was so in love. His name was Johnny, and we met in Bible study."

"Gag me," Fonu said, with a scrunched-up face. "Keep the anal details to yourself."

Gerry snapped out of his reverie and said, "Oh no Fonu, it never got sexual. I was much too screwed up to follow through with anything sexual. I just couldn't make sense of what the church leaders were teaching. They said what I felt was love was really sin, and I knew what that meant. It meant without God. It meant I would never get to grow old with the one I loved. It meant my feelings of love weren't really love. What were they then, evil?" Gerry asked, flashing the double horn sign with both hands, showing all his teeth and hissing like a demon.

"If you try, you might understand, I was bordering on crazy at the time. It was my own private insanity caused by human church leaders - not my brain chemistry. The gift was, my interest in psychiatry grew from the insanity I experienced in my own life. For me, studying psychiatry sounded like a good idea at the time."

"It obviously helped," Larry said, very seriously.

"Thank you, Larry. Yes, it did," Gerry said. "Studying psychiatry helped me realize, I wasn't crazy. Now, I see it as my special gift. I have an excellent career and my practice is flourishing. I'm very happy for the most part."

"Are you a specialist?" Donna asked.

"You said you were very happy, for the most part," Fonu Ali said. "What does for the most part mean?"

"Now I feel like I'm being interrogated," Gerry said, smiling anxiously and putting a finger to his lips.

"We all go through it," Don said. "Welcome to group therapy."

"Yes, I'm a specialist," Gerry said. "My specialty is helping gay men in a homophobic world."

"And why are you only happy for the most part?" Fonu pressed.

Gerry inhaled deeply, held it a few seconds, and then blurted out, "My patients don't know I'm gay." Then he inhaled deeply again and said, "I'm living a lie, and I'm all torn up inside. That's why I'm such a flamer here at home in San Jose with you guys. The rest of my life, once I hop on the train to The City, I pretend to be straight for the sake of my career. I'm deathly afraid of being outed."

"What? You're a gay shrink pretending to be straight while you're helping gay men maintain their sanity in a homophobic world?" Donna asked.

Gerry got all businesslike and said, "Yes, a lot of same sex loving people begin to question their sanity at some point, especially people like me reared in rigid as stone fundamentalist families. Thanks to the religious right my business is booming. And my advice is always the same. I tell my patients to re-read the *Sermon on the Mount* and think for themselves."

"That's excellent advice," Larry said. "I think everyone should re-read the *Sermon on the Mount* and think for themselves."

"I love the *Sermon on the Mount*," Donna said.

"My favorite," Don said, looking over at Donna.

"Mine too," Fonu Ali said.

"You know, if everyone read and understood and lived their lives like Jesus taught in the *Sermon on the Mount*, we'd have world peace," Don said.

"Who would have guessed our flaming gay neighbor was a closet Christian?" Fonu said.

"There're a lot of closet Christians nowadays," Larry said. "People turned off by homophobes with hot wives and false prophets for profit. People who feel like un-plugging from organized religion. People who don't want to listen to Bible bumpers with blinders on who can't admit they don't have a good answer for a gay person."

"I don't understand," Donna said. "If you're counseling gay men, why lie and pretend to be straight and live a double life? Why make it so complicated?"

"Look, if you're a hardwired gay man like me growing up in a homophobic household, you're not questioning your sexuality. You're questioning your sanity. I guarantee it. So, I did what I had to do to survive. I lied. And I felt so bad, I contemplated suicide.

"Then!" Gerry exclaimed, clapping his hands once for emphasis and opening his eyes wide. "You know Don's theory about how truly good ideas come from God and how important it is to have a good big goal?" Donna watched as everyone else nodded in agreement and was listening closely. "Well, my first good idea, my first good big goal became just not killing myself. My next good big goal became mental health, and with mental health as one's primary goal, one needs to be objective about what is, and what is not, sin in one's life."

"Ah yes," Don said. "That makes sense. Like a heavy drinker, who's thinking he might have a drinking problem, doesn't ask another heavy drinker for objective advice about his problem drinking. Similarly, a gay man looking for objective advice, doesn't hire a gay shrink who'll tell him that what he likes to do is perfectly fine, just as long as he's having loving thoughts at the time."

"Exactly Don. How could loving thoughts be bad?" Gerry asked.

"Only you know what's going through your own head," Don replied.

"I think you understand me Don."

"I try."

CHAPTER 14

The Question

"I can't imagine having loving thoughts while being boned in the ass," Fonu Ali said, with his face all scrunched up like he was smelling something bad.

"Quit making faces Fonu!" Don exclaimed. "But Fonu brings up an important point. Guys like us can't imagine having loving thoughts while being boned in the ass. So, it's very hard for us to accept the possibility of having loving thoughts at the same time as anal sex."

"Only you know what you're thinking when you're doing it down there," Fonu said, looking at Gerry with his face still scrunched up.

"And that's why we cut people some slack," Don said. "Because we can't read other people's minds."

"It's like, for me, I really enjoy drinking beer," Fonu said. Then, he paused and looked at Don. Don was looking at Fonu deeply, because Fonu was talking about their theory. It was an all-encompassing theory explaining sacred scripture, sin, and why gays will be in heaven too.

Fonu Ali continued, "My sin of choice is drinking too much beer on occasion."

"And..." Don said, still looking at Fonu deeply.

"And smoking weed too much," Fonu said. "And eating too much. Especially, when I drink and smoke weed too much. That's it Don! No more in mixed company."

"Okay Fonu," Don said, smiling. "Thanks for sharing."

Fonu smiled and said, "It's our theory, right Don?"

"Yes, of course Fonu. It's our theory," Don said. "We've been talking about it for several years now, haven't we?"

"It's been five years," Fonu Ali replied.

"You see, we all like to eat and drink," Don said. "And sometimes, we like to eat and drink too much. It's perfectly normal. So, we should just admit it."

"And smoke weed," Dave interjected.

"And have orgasms," Gerry said.

"Yes Gerry," Don said. "And all these things can be good and natural in moderation, but in excess they can also be bad. Therein lies the rub, because even something as good and natural as eating or sex can destroy a person's life. Therefore, how does one determine what's bad?

"One might say that anything in moderation is fine, or that it's all about time. So, as long as you're not wasting huge amounts of time doing what you like to do, then it can't be all that bad. But what about anal sex? Fonu and I asked ourselves this question as we studied everything gay, and we discovered something more important than time.

To simplify and help illustrate our point, we eliminate one human being from the sexual equation and substitute an effing machine. Then, we ask the effing machine question."

"Effing machine question?" Larry asked.

"What effing machine question?" Donna asked, with a look of doubt on her face.

Gerry perked up and scooted to the edge of his throne and asked, "Did you say effing machine? I got to hear this."

"Okay everyone," Don said. "This question will help explain our theory about sin and how sin is different for different people. Thinking about this question will help us understand the problem with religion too. And once the religion problem is solved, we'll be on the verge of attaining world peace and bringing sanity to gay people and people who want to accept gay people, not just tolerate them.

"Here's the question, and you need to get a mental picture before answering." Gerry was literally on the edge of his seat wondering what the effing machine question was. "Imagine two naked men," Don said. "One, a raging Bible bumper. The other, a flaming homosexual. Now, imagine both these men being thoroughly gratified by elaborate effing machines. Now, I ask you, what's the difference?"

"Only their thoughts," Donna and Larry answered simultaneously.

Don and Fonu were flabbergasted. They couldn't believe it. Both Larry and Donna got the answer right off the bat.

"I have a question Don," Gerry said.

"Yes Gerry."

"I'm still working on this mental picture. Are they both good looking naked men?"

"Yes Gerry," Don said. "They can both be good looking naked men if you'd like, but their looks have nothing to do with it."

"That helps a lot," Gerry said. "I see two good looking, large, naked men with beards. And what kind of attachments do these effing machines have? Are they milkers or piledrivers?"

"You have to use your imagination," Don said. "Never mind Gerry. Donna and Larry got it. The only difference is what they're thinking at the time."

"I can't believe they both got it right," Fonu said. "She doesn't look like the type that would."

"That would what Fonu? Understand the importance of our thoughts? Or know what Jesus taught? Or be a closet Christian? Or what, Fonu?" Donna yelled defiantly.

"That would really get it," Fonu said timidly, now a little afraid of the petite girl with a strong voice.

"Get what?" Donna said, thinking Fonu was just like the other disappointing men in her life. "What? That women should cook, clean, submit and keep their mouths shut?"

"Hold on there, Donna," Gerry said, coming to Fonu's defense. "These guys are very progressive. They're nothing like that. They sure are fresh air to me. Are you kidding, beer and imagining good looking, naked men on effing machines? I know Fonu's a little rough around the edges, but these guys are the best. You need to look inward honey. It's obvious you've been traumatized. You have a little pent up anger maybe? It's okay honey, we all do. Just let it out, let it all out, you can tell me anything," Gerry said putting his arm across her shoulder.

"I'm not letting anything out," Donna said assertively, pushing Gerry's arm off her shoulder.

"I'm sorry. I did it again with my big mouth," Fonu said, looking at Donna sincerely. "Not many people really get it. You know, the importance of our thoughts."

"Don't forget about Fonu's syndrome," Don said, looking Donna deeply in the eyes. "Nowadays, most young people never pick up a sacred book, let alone read it and try to understand it. Our theory helps people get it a different way, without all the brainwashing, that's all."

"And regarding gay acceptance," Fonu said. "Since it's impossible to imagine having anal sex with loving thoughts, our theory states for total gay acceptance, everyone must admit anal sex is bad. Heterosexuals and homosexuals, no discrimination, just don't mess with the base chakra when it comes to sex."

"Brainwashing?" Donna said, with a questioning look on her face.

"Oh yes, of course," Don said. "Call it patterned thinking if you want, same thing."

"I agree," Gerry said. "It's obvious half the world has been brainwashed into homophobia."

"And eating crap," Fonu Ali said.

"And believing sex leads to joy," Larry said.

"There's all sorts of brainwashing going on out there," Don said. "Once you really get it, you'll see brainwashing going on everywhere. At Church, in schools, on TV, but most of all at home. Parents teach their children to be just like them, effectively brainwashing them. It's obvious, but brainwashed people have children. And sometimes, brainwashed people have lots of children, and these children turn out brainwashed just like their parents. So, we need to break the cycle of brainwashing, or we'll never have world peace."

"Okay, now I'm following you," Donna said. "In my home there was a lot of attempted brainwashing going on all around us."

"Oh yes, brainwashing's been going on at home for millennia," Don said. "Just about everyone was brainwashed by their parents. Fundamentalists brainwash their kids one way. Atheists brainwash theirs another. If you were brainwashed fundamentalist growing up, most likely you're homophobic and rigid as stone in your beliefs."

"And if your father was a good, super moral atheist who never thanked God," Larry said, "most likely he was the one you worshiped growing up. That is, until he was knocked off his pedestal and you were woken up. It's similar to ancestor worship practiced by Chinese Buddhists. Either way, most of us were conditioned to believe exactly how our fathers believed."

"Unless you're gay with a fundamentalist father," Gerry said. "Then, either you think about suicide or rebel in some other way, like becoming a homophobic homosexual, and those dudes have some real hang ups. Married men who think about men while they're doing it with their wives. In my opinion, they're the worst. I know. I council several of them, and they all go to church."

"Gay acceptance wasn't part of the brainwashing in my home or at our Church," Donna said. "Our neighbor was gay, and we talked a lot, and all he wanted was true love. All he wanted was to find and marry his lifelong special someone. My father just grumbled and said, 'He can either choose Jesus or his promiscuous gay lifestyle. He can either choose life or end up dead.' But our neighbor was celibate."

"Attaching the label, 'Chooses gay lifestyle,' to all gay people is just plain mean," Don said, with quoting fingers in the air.

"And misleading," Larry said. "Like it says in Isaiah 9:16, 'The leaders of the people mislead them.' "

"And stupid," Fonu said. "Many get married for life. They're not all flamers like Gerry, all sex, sex, sex."

"Words are one thing big guy. My sex life isn't too exciting. How about you Fonu?" Gerry asked.

"How did we jump from brainwashing to my sex life?" Fonu asked.

"Leave it to Gerry," Don said. "Fonu, why don't you explain how we brainwashed people to lose weight."

CHAPTER 15

Money for Brain Surgery

"Okay Don. Where should I start?" Fonu asked, briefly pushing his lips out.

"I think you should start with Dave," Don said. "And how we needed money for brain surgery and therapy for him."

"Okay, well, like Don said, we needed money for Dave's brain surgery and therapy. Dave was really screwed up at first, even a partial lobotomy is pretty bad, huh Dave?" Fonu asked, as Dave smiled and nodded.

"I'll never forget it," Fonu said. "Dave came out of his coma on his eighteenth birthday. We were so happy to see Dave smiling, we had a party in his room. Then later that same day, Dave's foster parents abandoned him, and that's when Don had his good idea. Don said, 'This is it Fonu! This is it! This is our own special test, our own Bhagavad Gita story, our own special battle between the good and selfish ideas in our head. This is it Fonu!'

"Don had a good idea at the time, and he convinced me. We had to take care of Dave! If not, Dave would have to live some place with the insane. Don and I agreed, and that's when our lives really started to change.

"We had a good purpose in life, and the good ideas were flowing. Don's next good idea was auctioning off the race car he won in a robotics contest at the university. And that car was the hottest thing you've ever seen. It was a one of a kind, boron composite Tesla SR Race Edition, and that car lit it up like you wouldn't believe. It had a wicked five color air brush job and all the options. Don sold his most prized possession. It was the official pace car for the *All Electric Grand Prix*.

"Then, we pooled our money and bought this house. We buried two forty-foot bunkers in the back yard, converted them into hotel rooms and rented them out to artists and illegal immigrants. It was my good idea," Fonu said proudly.

"Undocumented," Don interjected.

"Sorry," Fonu said. "Undocumented illegals."

Don laughed and said, "Seriously, we have two starving artists and four hard working undocumented immigrants living out back underground. They help pay the mortgage, but it wasn't enough for Dave's brain surgery."

"And brain surgery is expensive!" Fonu exclaimed. "So, we needed a lot of money. Maybe you might think I'm weird, but I like watching church on TV. And those TV churches sure bring in a lot of money. The same thing with cults, and sometimes it's hard to tell the difference. So, we decided to start our own cult. It sounded like fun, and then we'd have all the money we needed for Dave's brain surgery."

"It sounded like a good idea at the time," Don said. "Maybe not one hundred percent good, because money was involved, but the money was going to a good cause, Dave's brain."

"Seriously, you guys started your own cult?" Larry asked.

"It's a weight loss cult," Fonu said. "And we're still growing."

"Does it really help people lose weight?" Larry asked.

"Yes, a little too well in one case," Don said. "Everyone lost weight, even Fonu at first."

"Then I reached a plateau, and I've been there ever since," Fonu said somberly, pushing his lips out and dropping his head.

"We brainwashed our cult members to love the feelings of hunger pangs," Don said.

"And it worked for everyone, except me," Fonu said. "I don't know why."

"Yes you do Fonu," Gerry interjected. "You just haven't uncovered it yet. Somewhere deep inside, you do know why. Oh, I'm sorry. I interrupted you," Gerry said, putting a finger to his lips.

"Our cult is different than most," Don said. "You see, most cults are bad because they erect barriers between the members and the rest of the world, especially family and friends. The unique twist with our cult is, the good friends and relatives of our cult members became our primary marketing force, because our members really did lose weight, and they really are happier.

"The relatives and friends of our members saw the changes with their own eyes. They saw we really helped their loved ones," Don said. "The result was, many friends and relatives became cult members too and lost weight. Then their friends saw them, and a chain reaction occurred. Our cult became a huge success. All it took was new habits, a new routine and good brainwashing."

"You use the term cult so freely," Donna said. "Does everyone know they're in a cult?"

"Yes, we called it the *Cult of Food and Dance Incorporated* for a reason," Fonu replied. "It was my idea for reducing liabilities. We had new members sign a waiver too, allowing us to brainwash them for the purpose of losing weight.

"And we love bombed our newcomers to enhance our brainwashing. And we had quirky little sayings, that became our own group speak. And, of course, we had Don our charismatic leader," Fonu said, nodding to Don.

"Most importantly," Don said. "Everyone in our cult had a common good big goal. In addition to losing weight, everyone had the good big goal of helping Dave. Once they saw the weight coming off, once they were feeling the love, they happily donated to the cause."

"You brainwashed them Don?" Donna asked in disbelief.

"They had to lose weight if it was going to be a successful cult," Don said. "So, we brainwashed them. I wasn't leaving anything to chance."

"How'd you do it?" Larry asked. "I know how hard it is to lose weight."

"You see, weight loss is all about time," Don said. "Most people eat because it's lunch time or dinner time. Therefore, it's time to eat. A lot of people eat, even if they're just barely feeling hungry. But that's the old brainwashing, from a time when people worked hard at manual labor and needed lots of calories.

"The new brainwashing simply suggests, why not wait a few hours and enjoy a few hunger pangs for a change? Why not exercise when you feel hungry? Why not do a few crunches on an empty stomach? We simply suggest people exercise a little when they feel hungry and wait a few hours before they eat. And when they do eat, our brainwashing helps people eat the good stuff and stay away from fast food.

"We showed people love and friendship by spending time with them. We listened to them and encouraged them to talk about their problems and their purpose, and we shared our good big goal of helping Dave get the brain surgery he needed. Mostly, we sang and danced around and a lot, like a bunch of over-weight Hari Krishna's. We'll have to give you a demonstration," Don said, as he pointed across the room to a blue door with beautifully painted red rooster on it. "In there, behind Fonu's rooster, is where it all started."

CHAPTER 16

Abe Seabrooke

A t that moment everyone could hear singing. It was getting louder and louder, and soon the words became very clear and everyone could hear, "I love carrots, I love apples, I love beets and cabbage too," as a very large white man, wearing a white beret, dressed head to toe in a white suit, came through the foyer and into the room. "I love the feeling of hunger pang," he sang as he glided his girth into the room with his arms out like an airplane and his palms to the floor. He had a white beard and a mustache that made his head look like a cross between Mark Twain and Colonel Sanders, but his body was much fatter. "Don, I feel like a million bucks today. What's going on? Having a party and I wasn't invited?"

"Abe, you're out of the hospital! Give thanks!" Don exclaimed, as he ran over and greeted him with a big hug. "Larry, Donna, I'd like you to meet Abe Seabrooke. Abe, I'd like you to meet our new friends Donna and Larry.

Larry's a fellow floater and a Bible bumper like you," Don winked at Larry.

"Any friend of Don's, I'm very pleased to meet," Abe Seabrooke said graciously, as he shook hands with Donna and Larry. "Why hello there Gerry. I'm surprised to see you here hanging with the guys."

"I'm just another one of the guys today, and its beer O'clock," Gerry said. "I just couldn't refuse the invitation. What about you Abe? Have you had your homophobic awakening yet?"

"Now that you mention it, I did!" Abe said, as he approached Gerry opening up his arms. "I had an awakening in the hospital. Come here Gerry, I have a big hug for you, you thin, dark, effeminate man you. Come to Papa."

Don and Fonu couldn't believe their eyes as they watched the two embrace. Fonu looked over at Don and said, "Could it be a homophobic awakening?"

"I believe miracles happen in hospitals," Don replied. "Let me give you all a little background on my friend Abe Seabrooke here. You don't mind, do you Abe?"

"Have at it Don," Abe replied.

Don spoke like a preacher fired up on stage delivering a sermon. He paced assertively, and then he stopped to deliver some words, "Abe Seabrooke here, who you all just witnessed hugging my gay neighbor Gerry, was formerly the senior raging homophobic pastor of one of the largest fundamentalist churches in San Jose." Don paced a few more steps, stopped, turned and said, "And it looks as if Abe has changed his homophobic ways. Can I get a witness?"

"I'm a witness," Gerry said.

"I'm a witness," Dave said slowly.

"I'm a witness, but I don't believe it," Fonu said. "Abe was more homophobic than I was."

"Like you're not now big guy," Gerry said.

"Only around you, because you're such a flamer," Fonu replied.

"Okay, okay, quit it you two," Don said.

"Yes, Abe really has changed since we met him five years ago," Don said. "Not only has he lost over a hundred pounds, it seems as if he's had a homophobic awakening too. This is so cool.

"Last week Abe passed out on the beach after floating. He ended up in emergency and gave us a real scare. He was out cold in a coma for four days, but now he's looking great and appears better than ever. I can't wait to hear about your awakening Abe, but first, I need to know why you passed out and went into the coma. What did the doctors say?"

"They said I poisoned myself by metabolizing my own toxic fat," Abe said, as Dave giggled a little hearing this.

"What? Did you stop eating all together?" Don asked, very seriously. "Did you stop eating your carrots, apples, beets and cabbage too? You know, it takes time to lose weight. We specifically brainwashed that into you. I'm not sure what happened?"

"I am!" Fonu Ali exclaimed. "This guy almost blew the whole thing!"

"You're right Fonu. I really blew it," Abe said, looking over at Fonu and then Don. "I ate nothing and drank only water for over three weeks, and it almost killed me. I didn't realize it'd been so long."

"It's great seeing you alive and well today," Don said. "And I love seeing you change. Last week you were homophobic and near death, and now only a week later, you're hugging my gay neighbor. It helps me believe world peace is possible."

"Yup, death can do it," Fonu Ali said, "or near death as the case may be.

CHAPTER 17

The Death of Fonu Ali's Father

"Death woke me up from my brainwashing," Fonu Ali said. "For me, it was the death of my father."

"Oh my word Fonu! I didn't know. I'm so sorry," Gerry said. "Let it out. Let it out."

"I am letting it out Gerry!" Fonu Ali exclaimed, looking at Gerry with a scowl. "My father was a strict Muslim, so that's what I was. He was killed during the Hajj of twenty-fifteen. You know, the pilgrimage required of all good Muslims once in their life?" Most everyone nodded.

"I was only twelve at the time," Fonu said, pausing to maintain his composure. "I saw my father get trampled in a stampede of people in white. That experience changed my life. It opened my eyes and mind, and I thought, maybe the Hajj wasn't such a great idea from God after all. You know, over two thousand people died.

"After that, I questioned everything I believed. I thought if the Hajj wasn't such a great idea, maybe some other things I learned from my father, that he learned from his father, and on and on, weren't all such great ideas from God. I started thinking differently, and from then on, I didn't just read the Quran, I studied it, and I thought a lot about what I read. And I read the Bible and the Bagvadt Gita too. I studied everything I could find about God, because I wanted to know what other people knew.

"I wanted to understand why my father died so tragically, and why I survived. I wanted to understand the purpose of mine and my father's life. I still believed in God, but I didn't know what to call God at the time. I was questioning everything, but I was still talking to God. I was still praying, but when I prayed it was like, why are you effing me so hard in the ass God? Why am I even still talking to you God? Am I crazy talking to some invisible thing out there? I know you're not the creator of insanity, but are you trying to drive me out of my freeking mind God? Or should I call you Allah? I don't think so! I was so angry at the time. I was feeling the insanity."

"Is it true in some Islamic countries, Muslim's aren't free to change religions," Donna asked.

"Sad but true," Fonu Ali said. "Eff that, I'm American. My father came from Afghanistan, and where he came from, they'll kill you if you even suggest they might be one percent wrong about what they believe. You know, regarding their strict Islamic crap. Don't even try warning them the Hajj might be dangerous.

"What I don't get is this," Fonu said, and he was emphatic. "My father believed Jesus was a prophet, but he never even tried to understand what Jesus taught. He refused to read the

Sermon on the Mount or anything in the Bible, dismissing it all as corrupted. That's what his father taught him.

"My father smoked cigarettes like he had a death wish, but he refused to accept the idea of original sin. He loved his laws written in stone, but he didn't understand, laws written in stone don't work."

"That's like the biggest theme from the Bible," Larry said. "Laws written in stone don't work. The spirit of the law is what matters. That's what Jesus taught."

"Why don't moderate Muslims speak up and condemn the terror attacks?" Donna asked.

"Because moderate Muslims have fundamentalist nutcases for relatives. Have you ever had a fundamentalist nutcase for a relative?" Fonu Ali asked, looking Donna straight in the eyes.

"Not a Muslim one," Donna replied.

"Then it may be difficult to understand," Fonu said. "They will considerate it their duty to kill you if you even suggest having a Bible study. Therefore, moderate Muslims don't say a thing. They don't want to be killed by some wacko relative coming out of the woodwork. So, they keep their mouths shut. It's as simple as that."

"There are a lot of nutcases running around on both sides of the field," Larry said.

Fonu Ali continued, "Well, I thought a lot about the Hajj after losing my father. I was so angry. The Hajj seemed so stupid to me. So, it seemed like a good idea at the time to study the Quran and try to figure out what was wrong. And as I studied the Quran, it became obvious, some things were inserted by humans. For example, the Hajj.

"It seemed obvious to me, the Hajj was inserted as payback to the big caravan companies of the time. And big travel is still raking it in, as millions of people travel to Saudi Arabia to participate each year. Don and I agree, anytime you combine human beings with a whole lot of money, you have a recipe for temptation, which results in greed and corruption."

"How'd you figure it all out?" Larry asked.

"I just read a little every day, and I took notes," Fonu said. "At first, I just compared the *Sermon on the Mount* to everything else I learned in Islam growing up. The concept of loving our enemies was huge. It was completely new to me. And the idea that hateful thoughts were as bad as hateful actions blew my mind. These ideas were nowhere to be found in the Quran.

"What Jesus taught made sense to me, because I'm a sinner, that's for sure, but what I didn't understand was why these important teachings were left out of the Quran? That was the mystery. So, after a few more years of open-minded thinking and study, I began to focus on the Bible and Buddhism more deeply. Then, my Mom and I moved to San Jose, and a new chapter in my life started when I met Don and Dave. Dave was an atheist back then, just like he is today. And Don still studies everything, especially everything people argue about, like me."

"And just like Donna and Larry were dropped into our life today," Don said. "Fonu was dropped into Dave and my life back then."

"Luckily he didn't land on you," Gerry said, with a devilish smile.

"Well, it helped me a lot having Don to talk to about supernatural stuff," Fonu said, scowling at Gerry. "And Don knew a lot, because of always trying to figure out where his cool dreams came from."

"Thanks for sharing Fonu," Don said. "Yes, death can have a huge effect on someone's brainwashing. The death of Fonu's father sure woke Fonu up, and I think Abe's near-death did it for him. You see, facing death, we tend to get very honest with ourselves. And, in that hospital, in that coma, you were facing death Abe.

"The fact that both Fonu and Abe made radical changes in their way of thinking is proof that Muslim and Christian fundamentalists can change their brainwashing and get re-brainwashed with love. I love it!" Don exclaimed. "If only people would communicate with other people who were brainwashed differently, rather than waiting until we face war, death and tragedy…" Don said, slowly shaking his head. "And speaking of brainwashing, I was just explaining our little group when you arrived Abe."

"You mean our little cult right?" Abe Seabrooke said, with a smile. "That's what the nurses and doctors were calling it. Do you realize, I was visited by more than a hundred very large, happy people? The strangest thing was, they were all singing the song. Remember when you and Fonu came to visit? Remember everyone softly singing the carrots, apples, beets and cabbage song? Singing that they love the feeling of hunger pang?"

"Yes, that was a little strange," Don said.

"Well, it wasn't just when you visited. It was all the time," Abe said. "People were singing in the waiting room and in my room, all week long. They were singing in the hallways and elevators, any time two or more of them came together, they started singing the song. The nurses and doctors told me all about it. They said the hospital never seemed happier. Carrots, apples, beets and cabbage, I love the feeling of hunger pang. Over and over they heard it, from over a hundred fat, happy visitors. When I came out of my coma and told them I hadn't eaten in three weeks, they got suspicious. They asked if I was in a fasting cult. I told them it was the *Cult of Food and Dance Incorporated*."

Don giggled a little, "Yes, I'd have been suspicious too. That song means a lot to us, but others can't relate. We associate that song with love, friendship and helping Dave. It sounds kind of crazy to everyone else."

"Yes, it sounded and looked a little crazy," Abe said. "Especially, since most of the people singing and dancing were over two hundred fifty pounds, gently poking each other, smiling and singing…poke me in the stomach, munch another carrot."

"I love the feeling of hunger pang," Don, Dave, Fonu and Abe all sang out in unison.

"All I know is, I've never felt so much love as in that hospital room being visited by fellow fat people. I've presided over thousands of church services, but I've never felt such love. Now, I believe differently. My near-death experience awakened me. It saved me. It saved my life in here," Abe said, putting his index finger to his chest. "So many thoughts went flashing through my mind. And like Fonu, after his father died, I started questioning some things my father taught me.

"Mainly, I was thinking about loving my enemy, and I felt so sad for Gerry. And I felt so bad! I realized, I made the Gospel unavailable to Gerry and a lot of other people who loved gay people. I asked myself, how would the gospel sound to Gerry coming from me? And the answer wasn't good. The Gospel I was preaching wouldn't sound like good news to Gerry. It would sound more insane. I was telling gay people the love they experienced, wasn't love, but something bad. I saw myself, and I listened to my words from Gerry's perspective, and then I felt something. I felt how it would be in Gerry's shoes listening to me. I'd want nothing to do with the love of God I was preaching. I'm so sorry Gerry. I feel like such an idiot," Abe said, getting a little emotional.

"Just like I felt earlier, in my gay pride outfit," Gerry said. "Oh Abe. Oh Don. Oh Fonu, I can't believe it, but I do," Gerry said, running over for a group hug.

"This is beautiful," Don said. "Seeing both extremes communicating and admitting their understanding was at least a little bit wrong, and now they're making up. It's like a perfect ending to a happily ever after story." *Maybe World Peace is possible?*

CHAPTER 18

The Weight Loss Cult

At that moment everyone heard a couple of knocks, and then, "Helloooo. I'm hungry," as a beautiful young woman entered the room, "but I love the feeling of hunger pang."

"Zola baby," Don said, as he stood up and walked over to greet her with a hug. "How you doing honey buns? And how's your grandfather?"

"Gramps is the same Don, thanks for asking. I just got back and came right over. How's Abe Don? I've been worried sick," Zola asked, with concern on her face.

"Why don't you ask him yourself?" Don replied with a wide smile.

"What?" Zola asked, looking across the room and seeing Abe rising from the big purple throne. Immediately, her face lit up and her white teeth shined out. "Abe Seabrooke, you large white man you. Give me some of that refined sugar you carry around everywhere you go."

"Zola darling! Seeing you makes my heart smile," Abe said, as they hugged.

"You look so much better than last week in the hospital," Zola said. "I came by to visit, but you were in a coma. I didn't think you could get any whiter, but you did. I'm so glad you're back with us and eating again."

"It must have been your visit that turned the tide for me," Abe said. "I'm eating carrots, apples, beets and cabbage, but I still love the feeling of hunger pang."

Don stood up and said, "Donna, Larry, and Gerry, I'd like you to meet Zola Jackson. Zola was one of our founding members, who's lost over forty pounds with our little group. Doesn't she look great! And Zola, I'd like you to meet our new friends Donna and Larry."

Donna and Larry shook hands with Zola, as Gerry stood by waiting for his introduction. "And this is Dr. Gerry Long, my gay psychiatrist neighbor. I don't think you've ever formally met. Gerry came over for a beer with the boys."

"Hello Zola," Gerry said, extending his hand. "It's a pleasure. I'm half African, but people say I look mostly Chinese, what do you think?"

"Nice to meet you Gerry," Zola replied. "I'm a good part African, but I'm one hundred percent American."

"That's what I love about Zola," Fonu said.

"Me too," Dave said.

"Hi Dave, you got a hug for me?" Zola asked with a flirtatious smile.

"You came by at the perfect time," Don said, as Zola and Dave embraced. "We were just about to demonstrate our little group's song and dance number."

"I'm so happy right now, I'd love to sing and dance some."

"Okay everyone, listen up," Don announced to the room. "We're going to demonstrate how we brainwashed people to lose weight. Actually, it was very simple. As in all cults, initially we love bombed them with friendship and camaraderie. Then, we practiced talk therapy. We shared our own issues, like our vices and guilty pleasures. We shared our problems and what we'd learned so far in life from our experiences. But mostly we spent time, the precious time required to get people to open up and talk about their stuff." Then Don raised his voice and said, "You know, we all need to talk about our stuff..."

"Or we'll stuff our face," Abe and Zola said in unison, like two thoroughly brainwashed cult members.

Don smiled, proud of his successful brainwashing. "Then, once we got them comfortable and talking, we listened to them deeply. And by listening to them, we loved them. We listened to their struggles, their gifts and dreams, and we encouraged them to cry if they felt like it.

"The key was getting people to open up and talk about the hard stuff. You know how it's hard to talk when you're emotional? You know how your lip quivers and you can't help but cry, right when you start to talk? So, it just seems easier not to talk about it and keep it all inside?"

"Oh yes, it's so very hard," Gerry said.

"What's so hard now Gerry?" Fonu asked with a scowl.

"To talk when you're emotional," Gerry said. "What were you thinking Fonu?"

"Yes, it's hard to talk when we're emotional," Don said, looking at Gerry and shaking his head. "But it's healthier to talk about the hard stuff."

"Or we'll stuff our face," Abe said.

"Yes, very good Abe," Don said, noticing how thoroughly brainwashed he was. "Once we got them talking and emotional, they became very receptive to our brainwashing, which was mostly dancing around, singing and having fun. Come on Fonu, strap it on brother. Let's show them how we do it."

"What?" Gerry asked, putting a finger to his lips, "Fonu's going to strap one on?"

"My guitar you pervert," Fonu said, scowling and making one of his faces.

"Comments like that turn us into homophobes Gerry," Don said, with a smile.

"Sorry, reflex mouth. My bad," Gerry said.

Don led the group towards the blue door with the red rooster on it. "I love Fonu's red rooster don't you?"

"Oh my word, Fonu!" Gerry exclaimed. "Your rooster is absolutely beautiful. Did you paint all these too?" Gerry said as he pointed around the room.

"I started painting after my father died," Fonu replied. "I haven't stopped."

"They're actually very good," Gerry said. "Artistic and musical. I'm impressed. If it wasn't for your weight problem, you'd be the perfect catch."

Behind Fonu's red rooster was a two-car garage converted into a music room. The walls had acoustic tiles, like in a recording studio, and the floor had wall to wall rubber cushioning. "Everyone, please come this way," Don said. "Kick off your shoes and join the fun. Dave, we need you on drums."

Don sat at the piano and started playing. Fonu came in on guitar and Dave kept the groove on the drums. Fonu started the singing: "I love carrots, I love apples, I love beets and cabbage too…"

Then all the cult members sang in unison, "I love the feeling of hunger pang." They continued dancing and singing, "Poke me in the stomach, munch a bunch of celery, I love the feeling of hunger pang."

Everybody danced. Everybody sang. Everybody poked each other gently in non-sexual ways. You couldn't help but smile. Zola moved closer to Dave and sang, "Poke me in the stomach," as Dave softly poked Zola's stomach.

"Munch another carrot," Abe Seabrooke chimed in, poking Dave's shoulder.

Then the whole group sang, "I love the feeling of hunger pang."

"Punch me in the stomach," Fonu sang, encouraging Donna to join in. So, she softly punched Fonu's large belly.

"Munch a bunch of celery," Zola sang out.

And the whole group sang, "I love the feeling of hunger pang."

Then Abe soloed, "I love carrots. I love apples. I love pickles and celery toooo."

And the group sang, "I love the feeling of hunger pang."

Then Don soloed, "Stab me in the stomach, much a tree of broccoli."

And everyone sang, "I love the feeling of hunger pang." They all danced. They all sang, and everyone was truly happy at that time.

The dancing, singing and poking went on for twenty minutes or so, and everyone got some good exercise had some good fun. At the end the session, Don announced like an MC at a special event, "Thank you all for joining in on our little love fest. We do this twice a day to help you get healthy, to help Dave, and to help anyone who wants to, lose weight. Thanks for coming, and please join us for refreshments. Like always, we have watermelon juice and of course…."

All the cult members yelled, "Carrots, apples, beets and cabbage."

CHAPTER 19

Fast the Demons Away

"Watermelon juice?" Gerry asked with his nose all scrunched up. "I thought we were having beer. I'm ready for a beer."

"Don't get your tutu in a bunch," Fonu said, with a scowl. "Don was just saying it like in group downtown."

"Of course, our sessions downtown are alcohol free," Don said. "We started this cult to help people lose weight." Then Don raised his voice and said, "And if you drink beer, wine or booze."

"You ain't never gonna lose," Zola and Abe said, responding in unison.

"Hey Dave, why don't you put that stew on," Don said. "And Gerry has a point."

"Okay Don," Dave said, as everyone else moved back to the circle of thrones.

"I'll do the beer honors," Fonu said, as he moved his three-hundred-fifty-pound mass toward the refrigerator. "How'd you like a partial bottle in front of you Dave?"

Dave shook his head, smiled and slowly said, "Full bottle in front of me please."

"I thought a partial frontal lobotomy was bad enough," Fonu said with a smile.

"You have a place downtown too?" Larry asked.

"Yes, we started out here with Zola and our founding members," Don said. "But after two years, we had thirty-three large, dancing people here, and it was getting crowded. So, we moved to a warehouse space closer to downtown."

"We danced, and we sang our silly song, but I think Fonu's produce was critical to helping people lose weight," Don said. "Fonu found the best carrots, apples, beets and cabbage and seasonal produce around."

"Have you ever tried to eat a cruddy carrot or a mealy peach?" Fonu said, with his lip all curled up. "They suck! Or a soft apple? You just can't eat it! So, what are you going to do if you're on the road, and you're starving and lightheaded? What are you going to do if all you've got is a mealy peach or cruddy carrot and you really need to eat? I'll tell you what you're going to do. You're going to stop at Jack in the Crack or Micky D's."

"And that fast food will kill you," Don interjected. "So, if you're serious about losing weight, you need to consider fast food places like crack houses and stay away."

"Good produce is hard to find, but the search is worth it," Fonu said. "Our carrots are juicy and bursting with flavor, and our apples are truly a joy to eat."

Don elbowed Dave, and in a slightly raised voice he said, "You need to keep good stuff around…"

"When you need to stuff your pie hole," Abe said, as Don and Dave giggled.

"We're up to two hundred forty-two members," Don said. "We have dance sessions twice a day, mornings and evenings, except on weekends.

"We buy over four thousand pounds of the best organic produce every week," Fonu said proudly. "We make a carrots, apples, beets and cabbage salad that's amazing, and our coleslaw, sauerkraut and seaweed surprise are beyond belief. And everything's been thoroughly tested and approved by me."

"It's surprising that singing a silly song and dancing around can successfully brainwash people to lose weight," Larry said. "I sure have tried a lot of nutty diets in my life, until I discovered fasting. Fasting helped me gain control over my food. And I discovered, fasting helps keep the demons away too."

"There you go, talking like an exorcist again," Don said.

"I know, people think I'm strange believing in demons," Larry said. "But don't you see, fasting is what you're helping these people do. Eating only fruits and vegetables is fasting. It's fasting from meat, fat, alcohol and refined sugar, the things our demons like us to consume. When we fast from these things, our demons get weaker, and we can't help but get happier.

"I've studied spiritual warfare, compulsions and demons," Larry said, "because I was compulsive in eating, drinking, drugs and sex. What I learned was, what begins as a guilty pleasure can grow into a compulsion. It's described beautifully in Romans 7:15, 'We don't understand why we do the things we hate and don't do what we really want to do.' It's the perfect definition of a compulsion.

"Then, our compulsion can grow into an obsession. At that point, our thoughts are completely wrapped up in our guilty pleasure. For example, a person with a lung infection, who's still considering having a smoke, is obsessed. I'll guarantee it, because their thoughts are being wasted thinking about that smoke. And that's Satan's big goal, for our thoughts to be wasted.

"An obsession can become demonic possession, and unless change happens, the person will soon be dead. Like someone smoking with a lung infection needs to wake up and realize they have a problem, a spiritual problem, because demons do exist."

"This guy does sound like an exorcist," Fonu said, making a face and looking at Larry.

"I performed an exorcism on myself and it worked," Larry said assertively. "I fasted for a week, drinking only water and reading only the Bible. I prayed, and I slept with a Bible under my pillow. I fasted, and I prayed, and I stayed away from my compulsions until most of my demons left me. All religions teach us to fast and pray, but they don't explicitly tell us why. I know why. It's to make the demons go away."

"Maybe they don't explain why, because they don't want to look like a nutcase saying that fat people have demons," Fonu said, now pushing his lips out with nothing else to say.

"All I know is, it worked for me," Larry said, lifting his shirt and patting his flat belly. "I used to be forty pounds heavier, because my demons loved pizza, beer, burgers and chips, not to mention drugs and risky sex. I still fast every Tuesday. I'm fifty-six, but I feel thirty. All it took was to stop the poisoning. And I realized, too much food is poison too!"

"Maybe we fasted the demons out of them. I don't know," Don said. "I think the human touch was very important, and the hugs people need to feel loved. When we sing, 'Poke me in the stomach' and whimsically poke each other, I think something special happens, something that breaks through barriers, like intermingling tunneling electrons. Then later, we can comfortably place our hand on someone's shoulder without a problem. It's only a theory."

"I love the hugs and our good big goal," Zola Jackson said, smiling at Dave. "I don't know what tunneling electrons do, but it feels like love to me. That's why I'm still here and getting tighter."

"You're right on with your good big goal theory," Larry said. "Not only for people who want to lose weight, but for anyone who wants to be their happiest and mentally healthiest. We all have goals, and most of us try to be good, but most of us don't have a good big goal.

"Early in life we focus on building a nest, attracting a mate and hopefully rearing some well behaving kids. Success in the material world is really our only big goal, because we're all focused on sex and survival, not unlike the birds or any other animal. But what's next? Once you have your fortified nest with twenty-four-hour wireless surveillance and guard robots, and a guard wolf to protect your wife, and a tank for her to drive, and a huge life insurance policy and a good education for your kids, what's next?

"Or, what if you don't have children and you find yourself with an excess? In both cases, you'll have a problem if you don't have a good purpose or a good big goal in your life. The question arises, what should we do with our precious time? Pursue a larger house? Amass more and more things we don't need to have? Sure, we could work on music or art, study science or do volunteer work, but most of us choose seeking pleasure rather than studying or working. It's only natural, like an animal.

"Are you an animal?" Larry said, with his eyes wide open to get everyone's attention. "Of course, there's nothing wrong with pleasure! Hell! We've worked hard and saved our money. We deserve it! The problems arise, when our own pleasure becomes our big goal in life, because there are good pleasures and bad pleasures."

"Playing music and singing are good pleasures," Don said.

"Same with making art," Fonu said

"Same with growing plants and playing drums," Dave said.

"Did you grow all these plants Dave?" Larry asked, tilting his head back, opening his arms with his palms toward all the plants hanging from the ceiling."

"I had help," Dave said.

"I love all the plants!" Larry said enthusiastically. "These plants are loved. I can feel it. You guys are impressive musicians too. It's too bad, most people believe making art or music is something only gifted people do. So, they dismiss the possibilities."

"People are being conditioned to believe more strongly in negative things," Don said. "People believe they can't experience miracles, or sing, or draw, or do math, or this or that. They believe strongly that they can't, but they refuse to think why other people can. It's a shame. So, rather than pick up a guitar or a paint brush, most people pick up a fork or a bottle, or they use drugs..."

"Or have promiscuous sex," Gerry interjected.

"Yes, Gerry," Larry said. "Sex is another thing we pleasure seekers seek. And, just like eating, sex is another pleasure that can be good or bad. Is sex good, just because it's safe? Is sex bad, only if you catch a disease, or get a girl pregnant accidentally? The definition of what's good and what's bad regarding sex is something people will be arguing about until kingdom come. One should take note, promiscuous sex being bad is one thing the big five religions all agree on."

"At least you admit it Gerry," Don said.

"Not me," Gerry said. "I was talking about my patients."

"Not you Gerry? Not ever?" Fonu asked. "Never had a rest stop rendezvous?"

"Well, not lately," Gerry replied, crossing his legs and folding his arms like a mental patient who doesn't want to talk about their stuff.

"Sex, drugs and alcohol are all pleasures we like," Larry said, "but eating is something we need to do to survive. This puts over-eating in a category all by itself.

"I'd put sex in the same category," Gerry said.

"Seriously," Larry said, "of all the destructive things we humans like to do, over-eating is the most innocuous and therein lies its subtlety. We all like eating something really good, don't we?"

"And drinking beer," Fonu said. "Anybody want another?"

"Yes, please," Dave said slowly.

"Beer me big guy," Gerry replied.

"Sounds good," Donna said, as she downed the last of her beer.

"What about you Larry?" Fonu asked. "Would the demon inside you like another?"

"Yes, we can have two, thank you," Larry replied.

"Beers all around," Don said.

"They don't talk about demons in church much, I'm talking about the demons we have inside us," Larry said, "because they cater to the masses. No protestant preacher in his right mind would ever say eating a doughnut was bad. No way. They're serving 'em up and our children are eating 'em like their favorite church activity. But some people, like me, need to stay away from doughnuts, because we have a demon inside who especially likes it when we eat donuts. It's the same thing with pain killers. Some people, like me, need to stay away from pain killers. I know if I feed my demons pain killers, it's going to get bad."

"This guy with his demon talk scares me," Fonu said, looking directly at Larry. "What? Do you think I have a demon in me that likes it when I eat meat and cheese sandwiches, heavy on the mayo?"

"It could be, if it's affecting your health," Larry said. "Is it?"

Fonu sat silently with his lips pushed out.

"This could explain some things," Don said. "It's subtle brainwashing, don't you see. Churches feeding kids donuts from the get-go. I'd like to see the statistics of denominational

obesity in America. Maybe the doughnut churches are causing America's fat kid epidemic?"

"That's the problem with the absolute interpretation of
the Bible," Larry said. "When the interpretation is wrong, it
doesn't help people. Like when Jesus said in Matthew 15:10,
'It's not what goes into one's mouth that defiles a person, but
the words that come out.' He didn't mean it's okay to eat like
a pig! He meant our words are much more important than
what we put in our mouths."

"Yes, what people put in their mouths should be their
own business," Gerry said, putting a finger to his lips and
looking at Fonu.

"Of course, because our words are the result of what
we're thinking," Don said. "Our thoughts are the most
important thing."

"Why would churches teach people to make poor food
choices like donuts?" Fonu asked.

"And teach people not to accept gay marriage," Gerry said.

"Short sighted pastors causing insanity," Don said.

"Blame it on the brainwashing?" Donna said, looking
over at Don.

CHAPTER 20

Blame it on the Brainwashing

"Why yes," Don said. "Blame it on the brainwashing. That is, if you want to keep talking, get along and be part of the solution. This is where we all need to take a hard look in the mirror and ask ourselves if we really want world peace? Or, is it more important for us to be one hundred percent right about everything?

"Take Fonu, for example. His father was a hardline fundamentalist Muslim homophobe, so that was Fonu's brainwashing until he was twelve. Add in his syndrome, and you'll understand why all sorts of insensitive words come out of his mouth. If you immediately take offence and shut him out of your life, you'll never see his art or hear him singing like an angel. You'll never get to feel his heart. Therefore, it's better if you blame it on the brainwashing, until you get to know him better."

"Like when someone referenced Leviticus 18:22, and said I was an abomination," Gerry said. "Should I have blamed it on his brainwashing and continued the conversation?"

"That person was plain mean!" Donna exclaimed.

"Using the Bible that way was bad!" Larry said. "Very bad."

"That person was a bully," Don said. "And bullies, by definition, rarely admit their mean words were wrong. Fonu, on the other hand, has no problem admitting he could possibly be wrong about something."

"I could possibly be wrong about a lot of things," Fonu said.

"That's what Don said when we met," Abe said. "That is, once he realized I was a fundamentalist. He said our different beliefs on important matters make us look crazy to each other. Therefore, in order to get along and keep communicating, he suggested we each blame it on the other's brainwashing."

"You see, once we understand we were brainwashed," Don said, "most of us will get a little angry, but that's the good kind of anger. Good anger can motivate us to study and help change things for the better. And since nobody was brainwashed perfectly, we should all be a little angry."

"I sure am angry," Donna said. "I feel like the world is trying to brainwash me to choose an extreme. Like, I either have to be a super obedient Christian sheep or against anything having to do with Jesus, and there's no room in between. I either have to be a homophobic asshole or an anti-Christ slut possessed by demons. I feel pressured to take a side, when I disagree with both extremes."

"Yes, just because I'm anti-bully and I'm okay with gay marriage, doesn't mean I'm pro anal. It's part of our theory," Fonu said, looking over at Gerry with a disgusting look on his face.

"Fonu! Stop making faces at Gerry!" Don exclaimed. "Your face will freeze that way!"

"Don?" Gerry asked, as he scooted to the edge of his cushion with his knees together and a finger to his lips. "Will you please explain more deeply how anal sex is part of your theory?"

"Yes Gerry," Don replied. "But first let's discuss the extreme choices Donna just mentioned, because it's critical to world peace. You see, when a person says, 'Either you believe like me, or you're the enemy,' I guarantee they're toast, because their words just stopped the conversation. And communication is necessary for world peace."

"Satan loves these either-or questions," Larry said. "Like, either we bomb them, or they will bomb us. So, we better bomb them first. Or, either we fight gay acceptance or accept anal orgies in the streets and the destruction of the family as we know it."

"As a gay man who wants true love, I sometimes think the gay activist extreme is hurting my acceptance," Gerry said. "I realize now, I shouldn't have come over in my gay pride outfit if I wanted to be accepted by regular guys like you. I see that now so clearly, and I'm so sorry I made you uncomfortable earlier, but please, I'm literally on the edge of my seat, please explain how anal sex is a part of your theory?"

"How about you taking it from here Fonu?"

"Okay Don," Fonu replied. "You see, one very important part of our theory is that sex should be accompanied by loving thoughts of the person you're having sex with. Like, a man having sex with his wife, should be thinking of her, not the good-looking dude next door. I think we can all agree that would be bad.

"And regarding anal sex, we don't discriminate. We don't care if it's two men, or a man and a woman. Don and I agree anal sex is bad. Even two women. Look, if a girl wants to strap one on and give it to another girl in the ass, that's bad. Can anyone imagine having loving thoughts while being boned in the ass with a strapped-on appendage? Not me. Oh, and if you've never done it, but go around talking like you're a sexual extreme accepting person, with the everything's fine with me attitude, even anal sex, I suggest you try it. Then you can tell me how pro-anal you are. It's simple Gerry. Are you having loving thoughts while you're being boned in the ass?" Fonu asked.

"My word," Gerry said, "You really are anti-anal, aren't you Fonu.

"I just can't imagine having loving thoughts during anal sex," Fonu said, with a sour look on his face.

"What about you Don? Where do you stand on anal acceptance?" Gerry asked.

"Anal acceptance!" Don exclaimed, with a what the hell kind of look on his face. "This is the first I've heard of it. What, is anal acceptance a whole new level of sexual extremist crap I have to be okay with now? If so, you can count me out. You can put me in the anti-anal category, because I think anal sex is bad. I know, because I experienced it."

"Oh Don. You've been hurt, haven't you?" Gerry asked. "Let it out. Let it out. It's okay. I'm board certified."

"Certifiable," Fonu said with a scowl.

"Oh Gerry. Shut the hell up," Don said. "I'm not anti-anal because I got it in the pooper against my will. I'm anti-anal because I tried it with my girlfriend, and I remember my thoughts at the time. All I was thinking was, I couldn't believe she was letting me do it. And I thought it was tight and slippery. But what I'll never forget was the look on her face, and the fact that she never wanted to do it again. That look told me how good she thought it was. And afterwards, all I wanted to do was hop in the shower."

"Look, I guarantee it!" Fonu exclaimed, looking around the room at everyone like this was a major point. "If you have anal sex, you're going to hop in the shower after, because it's dirty. It's not something you do and then just fall asleep with ass juice all over you. You're going to take a shower after, because it's dirty. And I'm not talking working on the car dirty, I'm talking about filthy dirty! The dirty that spreads diseases, and that's bad."

"Yes, we're pro-gay marriage," Don said. "And we're working really hard on it. But, we're anti-anal and anti-pro-miscuity too. Why do we have to fit a mold that says if we're pro-gay accepting, we have to be pro-sexual extreme everything? Why do we have to be pro-gay lifestyle, pro-anal, pro-promiscuity, pro-casual sex with strangers in public restrooms, pro teaching our children all the different ways humans can freak on each other and on and on."

"That's just as bad as the fundamentalists demonizing gay people, teaching hatred and creating bullies in the world," Fonu said.

"Look," Don said, in a slightly raised voice. "We've been dealing with bullies since high school, and we learned a lot. We learned that most bullies believed their holy book was without error. I'm talking about Christian and Muslim bullies, who believed their interpretation was without error too. Our theory states, one person's perfect interpretation of sacred scripture can't be perfect when applied to another person who is very different.

"This especially applies to the religious leaders at the top creating the bullies. You see, although people all over the world want to live in peace and harmony, the religious leaders at the top want global domination. Suicide bombers doing what their leader says are a perfect example of the stupidest bullies."

"Exactly," Larry said. "The leaders of this world, all the leaders, religious and political, don't really want us to understand what Jesus taught. They don't really want us to love our enemy or try to understand people who are different, because that would mean seeing things from the other person's point of view. If it was two gay people who wanted to get married, to love them would be to attempt to see things from their shoes. If the bullies or religious leaders ever did this, they would see how wrong they look to people like us.

"Imagine a gay man truly in love…" Don said.

"On an effing machine," Gerry interrupted, putting a finger to his lips, and his other hand between his legs like a woman who needed to pee.

"No Gerry," Don said. "No effing machines involved here. Get your mind out of the gutter. I was just sharing the time I tried to love my enemy. She was the girl I loved and got pregnant, but she never told me. She just aborted our baby and disappeared. Later, I found out about her abortion. Then I saw her kissing a woman, and I freaked out. I was so mad I nearly had a break down. I was mad at everything gay, and my anger really affected me. I didn't like being angry. So, I did like the *Sermon on the Mount* says, I tried to love my enemy. I imagined myself in a gay person's shoes."

"You Don?" Gerry asked. "You thought about trying the gay lifestyle?"

"No Gerry, quite the opposite," Don said. "I imagined being a gay person in love, who wanted to get married, be monogamous and spend the rest of their life with the one they loved. I imagined going to my priest and hearing that my love wasn't really love.

"If I was that gay person in love, that priest would've seemed like a bully to me. I concluded, if it's possible for two gay people to be in love, then it's possible some church doctrine might be wrong. I'm talking about agape love with loving thoughts. The selfless kind of love. You know, the gaping, wide open kind of love, like Gramps had for Gramma, except it's two dudes or two ladies. Fonu and I both believe it's possible," Don said.

"Yup, as long as anal sex isn't involved," Fonu said, looking at Gerry.

"That's right," Don said. "Can we all just agree anal sex can't possibly be done with loving thoughts? We think that's what the Bible was trying to teach, but somehow it got all twisted into the gay demonizing thing. And that Gerry, is how anal sex is a part of our theory."

"I have to disagree," Larry said. "However impossible it may be for us to imagine having anal sex with loving thoughts, for someone else it could be possible. In other words, you might possibly be wrong Don."

"What the hell?" Fonu exclaimed, looking at Larry with a thoroughly scrunched up forehead and a new disgusting look on his face. Then he looked at Don expecting him to say something, but Don was silent. Don was quietly pondering the depth of Larry's bold statement. Fonu sat quietly with his lips pushed out. Then he said, "Don, aren't you going to say something?"

Don waited, then he said, "At the moment, I'm enjoying the thick tension in the room."

"I've heard about Christians like you Larry," Gerry said. "Christians who believe anything and everything is acceptable in the marriage bed. You must be reformed Calvinist if you are pro anal?"

"I'm not pro anal," Larry said. "It's amazing how difficult it is to communicate when anal sex is involved. People tend to forget every word after anal sex is mentioned.   What I said was, for someone else, it could be possible. And what I meant was, anything is possible with God."

"Anal sex with loving thoughts?" Fonu said, with his face still contorted. "I can't imagine it."

"I agree, it's difficult to imagine," Don said. "It's more like domination."

"Or willing submission with full written consent, like in the dungeons in The City," Gerry said.

"My point exactly!" Fonu said emphatically. "Dungeon sex isn't love! You don't seem to get it Larry." Fonu was distressed. He looked at Don and said, "I don't know what happened today Don. You bumped into this old Bible bumper float meditating in the ocean and come home saying Muhammad had a point, like you had a whole new awakening, like now you have a whole new theory. And now you're actually considering the possibility of anal sex with loving thoughts? I can't believe it. It's like our entire theory is crumbling."

"Our *Insertion Theory* is perfectly intact," Don said. "I'm done thinking about all the possibilities behind door number three for now, if that's okay with you Larry?"

"Fine with me," Larry said. "If anyone's interested, I wrote a little tract called the theology of anal sex. It's all in there."

"No, I'm not interested in the theology of anal sex. Crap!" Fonu exclaimed.

"I'd love a signed copy," Gerry said. "Anything that shows anal sex in a positive light... well...could I get two? I'll keep one in mint condition for my collection."

"Collection?" Fonu asked, with an even harder look on his face.

"Please, I thought we were changing subjects," Don said.

CHAPTER 21

The Bully Patrol

"What do you mean, you've been dealing with bullies since high school?" Donna asked, looking at Don. "You're so smart, Fonu's so big and Dave's so strong and cool, I can't imagine anyone messing with any of you." Dave smiled hearing this from the cute blonde damsel in distress.

"I'm not sure everyone wants to hear bully patrol stories right now," Don said.

"Sure we do," Larry said.

"I'm going to need another beer for this, anyone else?" Don asked, as he went to the fridge. "Dave, another partial?"

Dave nodded with his thumbs up. Then he said, "Yes please, Don."

Don handed Fonu a beer, and said, "Go ahead Fonu, you tell the story."

"Where should I start?" Fonu asked.

"Beginning," Dave said with a big smile. Dave loved hearing stories of the times before his lobotomy. He especially loved the bully patrol stories.

144 | D A V I D D E W A R R O B E R T S

"Well, let's see. It was twelve years ago back in high school. We were all sixteen and just starting our junior year," Fonu said, scratching his head trying to remember. "And as I recall…, the bully patrol all started because Don had a crush on a girl. Her name was Trina Covina, and she was beautiful and thin. We didn't know it at the time, but Don found out later, Trina was a lesbian."

Don cracked his beer, held it up and said, "Here's to Trina and good thoughts."

"To Trina and good thoughts," everyone said, as they toasted.

"Trina was super active and full of energy. She had gorgeous dark eyes and beautiful dark skin like me," Fonu said, pointing to his eyes and dark forearms. "She rode a skateboard, batted over five-hundred on the softball team, and she threw hard like a dude. But other than sports, Trina was very quiet, and her group of friends was a very odd group.

"Trina's friends were... how do you say... very different. And, you know how bullies enjoy picking on people who are different? Well, Trina's friends were a motley crew of social outcasts, and some bullies got their jollies giving her friends a hard time.

"The outcasts included Elly and Ally, the pitcher and catcher on Trina's softball team. And Tony and Franky, two thin gay guys," Fonu said, looking over at Gerry. "And you know how bullies love giving thin gay guys a hard time."

"Yes, I do Fonu," Gerry said. "I'm sure it was very hard. You have my full attention, please continue."

"Cindy was another outcast who spelled her name S-I-N-D-Y. She had bad acne and usually had blue green hair. She was skinny with lots of piercings and full sleeve tats. And Sindy always wore black.

"And there was Fredrick, who hated to be called Fred. Fredrick was a Filipino guy who always wore black too and hung around Sindy all the time. He pretended to be straight, but everyone knew he was gay.

"And lastly, there was Karen Henderson, Trina's best friend and next-door neighbor. Karen was a crack up and she always made people laugh, but her teeth were too big, and she was too fat, and she wore super thick glasses, so she looked odder than normal. And, you know how bullies love picking on people who look odder than normal? Well, Karen Henderson looked a little odd, but she was the nicest person you could ever meet, and Trina was Karen's protector.

"Trina's circle of friends were all social outcasts. They were either too gay, too different or too fat. Only Trina got a pass, because she was pretty, talented, thin, and nobody knew she was a lesbian. So, she never got harassed.

"Don liked Trina a lot and wanted to get to know her better. So, we moved our circle of friends closer to Trina and the outcasts. Don talked with Trina briefly, but he kept getting cock blocked by Elly, the pitcher on the softball team. Elly liked Trina too.

"As we got closer, we heard the bullies as they walked by. We could hear their harsh words, and this really bothered Don and Dave. They felt they needed to do something about it. And that's when Don had a good idea!

"Don's good idea was to impress Trina Covina by taking on the bullies with his words and his brain, with Dave and I backing him up with our muscle. *The Bully Patrol* was born. And together we took on the bullies.

"So, the next time Big Billy Badass and his two cohorts walked by and said, 'Butt munchers,' to Tony and Franky, the bully patrol went into action. Don walked right up to Big Billy and said, 'What was that dick-wipe?'

"This surprised Big Billy. He pretended to not hear Don's dick-wipe comment. 'What's up Don?' Big Billy said.

"Then Don said, 'Billy, your words reveal your thoughts which reveal your heart. Do you realize that? And do you realize, you pick on people weaker than you are? And do you realize, people are really hurt by your words? Well, now you're going to have to deal with me.'

"Big Billy accused Don of standing up for a couple of fags, so Don said, 'They prefer the term gay as long as it is not followed by the word boy.'

"Big Billy said, 'Either way, they're an abomination. My Dad said so, and it's in the Bible.'

"Don said, 'Isn't the main theme of the Bible thinking of others? Well, I'm thinking of Tony and Franky right now, and I think you hurt their feelings. So, you better apologize or it's going to get bad.'

"Big Billy said, 'I don't have a beef with you Don.'

"Don said, 'I have a beef with you Billy, and you should consider it on!' Don walked forward with his fists up. It was great, because Don's a lover not a fighter." Fonu was all excited telling the story.

"And remember what you said Dave?" Fonu asked, looking at Dave.

"I said, 'And if Don has a problem with you, I have a problem with you too.' "

"And then I said, 'And if Dave has a problem with you it is on.' So, we all walked forward ready to fight. Then I said, 'Billy, I'm going to put your head in my arm pit until you pass out, unless you apologize right now.'

" 'Anything but that Fonu. Sorry dudes,' Big Billy said to Tony and Franky.

"Big Billy backed down!" Fonu said, slapping his thighs once for emphasis. "And then Don gave Big Billy a lecture. Don said, 'Hey Billy, they've studied bullies who pick on gay guys. You should research it. Most bullies are actually wrestling with their own same sex attraction. I can't say it's true for you Billy, because only you know what you're thinking. But one thing's certain, when you're a bully, you look like an ass-wipe to the rest of us, including the girls. But I guess you're not into girls, are you? And that's perfectly okay Billy. I'm not going to judge who you love. But I suggest you stop being a bully right now and read up on it, because you need therapy man.'

"We were immediately heroes with Tony and Franky and Trina and the outcasts," Fonu said with a smile. "It was such a great feeling when Big Billy backed down. Later, we stood up for some Muslim girls wearing head scarfs, Sikhs wearing turbans and Jews wearing skull caps. We didn't discriminate. If anyone was getting harassed for wearing some identifying religious garb, the bully patrol went into action. It didn't take long, and by the end of the year, people felt safe again. The bullies backed down, and Don became the campus hero and Trina Covina's new best friend."

"Most bullies aren't too bright," Don said. "All that's needed is for someone to stand up to them, ask psychological questions and have a couple of big, strong friends backing them up."

"Jesus' good idea was not teaching people to wear religious garb like targets on their forehead for the bullies of this world to home in on," Larry said.

"You guys are like superheroes," Donna said. "How'd I get so lucky?"

"Luck?" Don replied, giggling to himself. "You were rescued by this happy man driving his tow truck from outer space." Don looked over at Larry. "Who thinks he's on a mission from God, who I bumped into floating in the ocean today, and now you're here. I don't think luck had anything to do with it Donna. You're here for a reason. There are no odds for something like this."

CHAPTER 22

You Can do Better Tomorrow

"Mission from God?" Abe Seabrooke asked. "That's your rig out front?"

"It sounded like a good idea at the time," Larry said.

"Did you say it sounded like a good idea at the time?" Abe asked, turning to look at Don.

"I know," Don said, nodding and looking back at Abe intensely.

"I must hear this one," Abe said. "What's the story Larry?"

"Well, my story really began after my wife left me for a woman," Larry said. "I told you Don."

"I know," Don said. "Go ahead Larry, share with everyone."

"It was love at first sight for me, and it only got deeper with time," Larry said affectionately. "We both surfed and loved to sing. She played the drums, and I played piano. We had so much fun. I felt in love and happily married for fifteen years. Then came the fateful day I found her birth control pills, and everything in my life changed. I thought we were trying to have a family.

"I asked about the pills, and she told me everything. She said she was done being tormented, so she left the pills out for me to find. She said she was done living a lie. She apologized sincerely as she told me she was leaving me. We both cried as she explained she was a lesbian, and she'd been on birth control pills the whole time.

"Without her, I felt like a boat without a rudder. I felt all alone in a town with a million people. I was depressed and feeling like crap. So, I quit my job, which left me with way too much time on my hands. I filled the void I felt inside. I numbed the pain. I kind of went nuts using prostitutes, alcohol and drugs. I just wanted the pain to end. I was feeling so bad. I felt like my dream of having a family was over. It was like I didn't have a purpose in life anymore, because for me family was everything.

"My wife was loaded and very generous in the divorce, but the money I received turned out to be a curse. I could have eaten at the best restaurants, drank and drugged myself silly every day and used prostitutes twice a week for thirty years with the money I had. But, in the end, after two years of pure hedonism, I realized it didn't work. I realized, pleasuring myself wasn't making me happier. It only made me feel worse.

"I used to believe love could conquer all, but I didn't believe that anymore. I was so angry she was a lesbian, but somehow I knew the people at my church demonizing her were wrong. I was hit hard with the reality of my experience. I was questioning the very core of my beliefs.

"Even though we went to church regularly, I really didn't get it. I really didn't understand the Bible's main themes until after she left me. It took me getting really drunk and crashing my car into my neighbor's tree and nearly killing his kid. The next day, I had an awakening. I looked in the mirror, and all I could see was my badness. I'd been going to church for fifteen years, but in reality, I had been worshiping her.

"I thought I understood the Bible, but I really didn't. At that moment I did. I finally got it! It finally made sense! I finally understood, because I finally knew I was bad and needed forgiveness. In the mirror, I saw all my crap, not hers. I saw all my badness clearly. I made my hot wife my idol, because she was like my God. She made me feel fearless and strong, like I could do anything by her side. She made me feel special. She made me feel proud of who I was, and then she was gone."

"I think most men worship women more than God," Don said. "You shouldn't beat yourself up so much."

"What saved me was seeing the reality of the pleasure-seeking person I was. I saw clearly into my *Mirror of Badness*, and at that moment, the Bible finally made sense. I finally understood why Jesus had to die. It was for me to understand I was forgiven and loved so much, and I had a life worth living." Larry smiled and made eye contact with everyone.

Then Larry got all animated and said, "I had this incredible understanding right? And it was then, I heard a small voice inside my thoughts tell me, 'You can do better tomorrow,' and then I got really happy. Of course I could do better tomorrow! It sounded like such a good idea at the time!"

Everyone was riveted on Larry's words. "Then, I just knew I needed a good purpose in life. I'll never forget it. I prayed until I fell asleep that night. I prayed hard and long. I asked God for another really good idea, a truly good purpose, to save me from what I'd become. I needed something new. I needed something good to replace all the bad I felt.

"Then, the next day, I woke up to the bombings and fires of 2025. I was home alone watching it on the TV news. I'll never forget. I still have those images in my head. Images of people jumping out of buildings, rather than burning to death. I heard over and over that day how they lacked the rescue equipment they needed to save all the people that were dying. It woke me up. I realized people were suffering, like Buddha taught. Some were still alive and suffocating as I watched. Then it hit me like the best idea to ever pop into my head. It sounded like a good idea at the time to spend my multi-million-dollar divorce settlement on my own personal rescue vehicle. So, I did it. I spent over three million on the rig and all the equipment outside."

"Are you suggesting the terrorist bombings of 2025 where an answer to your prayer?" Don asked.

"Yes Don," Larry said seriously. "I see the looks on your faces. Yes, everyone thought I'd blown a brain gasket. It sounds crazy I know. How could a terrorist act be an answer to prayer?"

"That means all the people that died were angels," Don said. "Same with all the Jews, Poles, Slavs, gays and disabled people murdered during the holocaust. All angels. It's another theory I'm working on. A theory in which we have a lot of angels walking around here on Earth. Oh, I interrupted your story, sorry."

"My friends and family sure couldn't understand," Larry said, "but I received a gift that day. The gift was, I didn't care what people thought anymore. I felt so free, maybe even a little happy crazy. I had a new outlook, like I was on an important mission. A mission that needed me to stop using drugs and prostitutes and getting drunk. I couldn't afford it anymore anyway.

"At first, I only saved cats from some really mean trees," Larry said, looking at Dave with a smile. "It took two years before I had my first human life rescue. It's been four years now, and little Julia Campos was my fourth. She's in intensive care in the burn unit right now."

"And you believe your good idea was from God?" Abe asked.

"With God, I prefer to say," Larry said. "Yes, I thought so then, and I still think so today. Maybe I am a little crazy, but I'm happy. I believe it was a truly good idea. I can't find any selfishness in it. You know, spending millions on a rescue vehicle, living in it, and driving around helping people, isn't something one does to impress the ladies.

"My theory is, purely good ideas are conceived with God, as opposed to other not so good ideas, conceived without God. In Spanish it's very clear. In Spanish the word sin means without. If I'm wrong, I may be a little crazy, but inside here," Larry said, pointing to his heart, "I found the joyful place."

"Maybe a little of each," Don said. "That's perfectly acceptable behavior around here." Don realized the depth of what Larry just said about sin.

"Sin means without in Spanish?" Fonu asked.

"Yes Fonu," Dave said slowly. "Like sin semilla, means without seeds in Spanish.

"So, sin is an idea or something we do without God," Zola said. "That makes sense."

"As opposed to a truly good idea or a good purpose," Don said. "Where somebody else benefits. The bully patrol was a good idea for the people being bullied and for our school, but it wasn't a purely good idea, because the end goal was only to impress a girl. It definitely wasn't all good.

"And Larry, even if you only saved one person, it'd be worth looking a little crazy," Don said, putting his hand on Dave's shoulder. "How else but, with God, could Fonu have come up with a carrots, apples, beets and cabbage brain-washing song?

"God makes different kinds of animals and trees, and it's obvious, God makes different kinds of people too, like Larry, with different good ideas and different dreams. And we need all these different people, so we can learn what we're here to learn. God makes atheists, because we need good atheists who believe religions are the problem in the world. And God makes radical environmentalists too, whose purpose is to protect mother earth, but is their purpose truly good? Only the person knows what's going on in their own head.

"We need animal activists, and people who trap and neuter feral cats. We need people who help the homeless and people who believe in saving the whales..."

"But if a man is only saving whales," Larry interjected, "as part of his big plan of having sex with as many whale loving girls as he can..."

"Then he's really not such a whale lover, is he?" Don said.

"He's just another person who believes sex will lead to the joyful place," Fonu said.

"A lot of people believe the lie," Larry said. "It's a big theme from the Bible. The whole business about circumcision was to explain that sex is not the end all for achieving joy."

"I think circumcision's barbaric," Gerry said.

"Anybody hungry? We have carrots, celery, cabbage, chicken and pea stew," Dave said slowly, as everyone got up from their thrones and moved to the kitchen table.

"Thanks Dave, no stew for me," Zola said, as she went around the room hugging people goodbye. "I'll have a couple of carrots and an apple when I get home, but right now I'm enjoying my hunger pang. I'll give thanks with you and see you all shining at eight Monday."

"Okay honey buns," Don said. *These people really need to eat some protein, maybe carrots, apples, beets, cabbage and protein powder?*

Dave ladled out the stew to the seven of them around the big kitchen table. Afterwards, he slowly said, "No matter what you believe..."

Then everyone said, "Give thanks."

"See you all shining at eight," Zola said, hugging Don, Dave and Abe as she left.

And everyone said, "See you shining Zola."

"No big pieces of chicken for me," Abe Seabrooke said.

"You should eat some chicken," Don said. "You need the protein."

"I'll eat what I'm served," Abe said defiantly. "There's protein in the broth. Please Dave, no big pieces of chicken for me."

As Dave served the stew, he noticed Donna looked troubled. Her eyes were pooling, and she was trying hard to hold back the tears. "What's wrong Donna," Dave said, as everyone's attention shifted to her.

"Nothing. Nothing's wrong," Donna said, shaking her head. It was obvious, something was wrong.

"Wait, wait what's up their honey?" Don asked, as he came over and put his arm across her shoulder. "What do you mean nothing? I can tell there's something."

"Larry rescued me too," Donna said, trying to be strong, but feeling really hurt. "For the first time in my life I felt safe and comfortable, like in an almost normal family. Then, I felt forgotten. I'm feeling a lot of mixed emotions right now." Donna looked at Don and broke down for a little crying spell.

"Of course, Larry rescued you too sweetie," Don said. "He was just counting people who would have died if he wasn't there."

"I feel like he saved my life," Donna said.

"I'm so happy Larry rescued you," Don said, looking into Donna's wet eyes. "I'm really happy you're here right now."

"Really Don?"

"Oh yes," Don said. "And it's okay to cry too. It's always good to talk about it, and it's okay to show your soft side. We all need to talk about our stuff…"

"Or we'll stuff our face," Abe Seabrooke said, with his mouth full of stew. Don looked at Abe and smiled, and Donna smiled too.

"I'm sooo happy you think of us as an almost normal family," Don said, with a gentle smile. "I feel almost normal, how about you Fonu?"

"I feel almost normal too. I just need to lose weight," Fonu said, looking at his belly. "I think I have body dysmorphia."

"Or a demon," Dave said, giggling.

"Maybe the brainwashing doesn't work on Fonu because he wrote the song?" Gerry suggested.

Donna smiled some more. She turned to Larry and asked, "Can we visit Julia in the hospital?"

"Of course, we can," Larry replied.

"I don't know why I'm so emotional," Donna said, as she began to devour her stew. "Um, um, um," she hummed as she ate and ate. "This stew is sooo good Dave. Um, um, um."

"Good for you too," Dave said slowly, as everyone ate.

CHAPTER 23

Fonu's Sandwich Demon

"Oh my, this stew is abtholutely wonderful Dave," Gerry said with a lisp.

"Abtholutely wonderful?" Fonu lisped back, sounding like Daffy Duck.

"I think so Fonu, don't you?"

"I thought you were going to man up," Fonu said, looking at Gerry directly. "Try saying, this stew is really good, and without the lisp."

"You can't lisp the words really good," Gerry said, slowly stirring his stew, holding his spoon with his pinky extended. Then he took a bite. "Um, um, um, oh wow, umm, umm umm. Yes, I can't believe it. Um, um..."

"It sounds like he's having sex with his stew," Fonu said.

Don looked at Gerry, who had a guilty look on his face. "It's because I'm gay isn't it?" Gerry said. "You didn't have a problem when the pretty young thing was doing the um umming and moaning and groaning. And you can't have body dysmorphia Fonu. That's when normal sized people think they look fat, so they lose weight and become thin, but they still think they look fat. You really are fat Fonu."

"But I don't think I look fat," Fonu said. "Isn't it the same thing?"

"It's similar, just flipped around inside your brain," Don said.

"All eating disorders are a symptom of mental illness," Gerry said, "because they're self-destructive. A person could be starving themselves to death," Gerry looked over at Abe, "or eating themselves into disability," now glancing at Fonu. "The root cause is always in their head. A father using the term chubby to distinguish between his two daughters, can cause his heavier daughter to see herself as chubby in the mirror for the rest of her life. Anorexia could be her cause of death."

"Words are so important," Don said.

"Or a father's harsh words to your mother," Fonu said. "My father always said my mother was fat enough already, and if she got any fatter he'd divorce her. He weighed her every Sunday and graphed the data on the bathroom mirror. I loved my father a lot, but not that part about him. She was big boned and Tongan. She was beautiful, but he called her fat. It was enough to give her a complex. When he got killed, we both got even fatter."

"That's fascinating Fonu," Gerry said. "So, you got fat too because you really loved your mother. It's classic Freud, don't you see? Subconsciously, you wanted to spite your father because of his name calling. Have you ever heard of the Oedipus complex? That's when a man subconsciously wants to kill his father and have sex with his mother, like in the ancient Greek tragedy, *Oedipus Rex*."

"What a great story!" Don exclaimed. "Written about 430 B.C. by Sophocles, it's main theme was the flawed nature of humanity."

"Score one for original sin," Larry said.

"I didn't want to have sex with my mother, you pervert," Fonu said, with a deep scowl and a new mean look on his face.

"Of course, you didn't Fonu," Gerry said. "But it might explain your weight problem. I think it's a psychological breakthrough. Maybe now you'll finally be able to lose weight. Isn't that one of your big goals?"

"Saying I have a complex doesn't help," Fonu said.

"I didn't mean to label you with a perverted complex Fonu," Gerry said, putting a finger to his lips.

"But you did Gerry," Don said, "and that's not going to help Fonu. I know. I've been trying to help Fonu lose weight for years. I've come up with all sorts of diets for him. First, it was the *Carrots, apples, beets, cabbage and chicken diet*, but that didn't work for Fonu."

"I never broke the rules," Fonu said.

"I know Fonu," Don said. "You never broke the rules. You just exploited them. That's why it's impossible to write a diet law in stone for an over-eater like Fonu. On the *Carrots, apples, beets, cabbage and chicken diet,* Fonu would eat two entire fried chicken's every day. And you know, the more you deep fry…"

"The sooner you gonna die," Abe replied in auto mode.

Don smiled and said, "The next diet we tried was the, '*All about time diet*,' or the '*Carrots, apples, beets and cabbage after 2PM diet*.' This diet works for most over-weight people, who eat too much too late, but it didn't work for Fonu," Don said, looking at Fonu. "Most over-weight people won't sacrifice sleep to get up at 3AM and eat. But Fonu really loves to eat, even more than sleeping, and he's a real binge eater too. Tell everyone what you did to keep gaining weight on the *Carrots, apples, beets and cabbage after 2PM diet*."

"I would get up at 3AM and fry some chicken or make myself a couple of meat and cheese sandwiches, heavy on the mayo, and eat until I was full and then go back to sleep. My two big weaknesses are fried chicken and meat and cheese sandwiches heavy on the mayo," Fonu said, lowering his head.

"At least you admitted it," Gerry said, in a supportive way. *This little group of friends was functioning like a very successful therapy group.* Gerry was very impressed with the healing going on around the table.

"You may have a demon in you, that likes it when you eat fried chicken and meat and cheese sandwiches heavy on the mayo," Larry said.

"You sure are strange Larry," Fonu said. "Can we please change the subject from talking about all my weaknesses?"

"I don't think we've discussed all your weaknesses yet Fonu," Don said, with a smile.

Gerry was raising his hand like an excited child waiting to be called on. "Yes Gerry?" Don asked.

"I'd like to hear more about Abe's near-death experience, and his homophobic awakening."

"So would I," Don said, looking over at Abe. "That is, if he's ready to talk about it?"

Abe Seabrooke was in deep thought. *Should I tell everyone everything? Fonu was brave enough to talk about his embarrassing binge eating disorder, and he bared his soul about his father's tragic death. Maybe it's safe to tell everyone everything?*

CHAPTER 24

Abe's Awakening

"Yes, I'll share," Abe replied, closing his eyes to think for a moment. "Looking back and connecting the dots, I can see my awakening started when I met Don, Fonu and Dave on one of my walks."

"You make it sound like you were out exercising," Fonu Ali said. "As I recall, you were on your ass."

"Yes, I was Fonu, but I'm embarrassed to announce that to the room."

"You know Abe," Don said. "We gotta talk about our stuff or…"

"Or we'll stuff our face, I know Don. I've shared this with you and Fonu, but if everyone must know, I was on one of my walks to get more beer and food. I was a hundred pounds heavier than I am now, and I was depressed. My feet were hurting, and my knees were bad and getting worse. And I had just been fired. I was the senior pastor, and the church was my life. I felt like a complete failure at the time.

"I was fat, and I knew it, just like all fat people know it," Abe said, looking over at Fonu. "And I knew I was getting fatter too, because I was punching new holes in my belt, and my belt was the only thing holding up my pants. It was so sad. I couldn't button my pants. I felt so bad.

"I was questioning my belief. How could I eat and drink so much if I really had the Holy Spirit in me? I thought maybe I wasn't saved, or like Larry, maybe I had a demon in me? And to top it off, the new senior pastor was so damn lean and good looking!

"For six months, all I did was eat, drink and watch church on TV. I was living in sweatpants and eating and drinking like I had a suicidal death wish.

"Then came the fateful day I fell in the grocery store, and I was too fat and disabled to get up. That was the day I met Don, Fonu and Dave. They helped me up and helped me home. They were complete strangers, but they were there for me. They rescued me," Abe said, getting a little emotional.

"And wow, look at you now!" Don said, in his encouraging way. "In only five years, you've lost over a hundred pounds, and you awakened to the fact that you really were a homophobe. You seem to have found some joy too. I remember how depressed you were. No wonder, eating junk, getting drunk and watching church on TV," Don said, shaking his head slowly in amazement. "Choose your poison. Your career was your life, and your life was the church. They canned you, and you were still watching church on TV. I can understand being depressed and eating and drinking too much, but I can't relate to watching church on TV."

"I like church on TV too," Fonu said.

"People sure are different," Don said.

"It's part of our theory," Fonu said. "God makes people different, to give us the opportunity to love them. It's the same reason He allows people to get sick, be disabled and grow old and feeble, to give us the opportunity to love them."

"And having people around who are different is a lot more fun too. Just imagine if everyone was a hardwired heterosexual fundamentalist," Don said, stretching his mouth with his eyes wide open in horror. "The world would be a very boring place. Obviously, that's not what our creator intended, because people were made like Gerry and people were made like Abe, very different."

Abe thought, *little does Don know,* and then he said, "I was so depressed. I felt like I was losing my grip. And then, when I slipped and fell and couldn't get up, I couldn't believe it. I was so embarrassed. I needed to be rescued by complete strangers, because I was too fat and disabled to get up. It took me falling in public, with everyone seeing me, to finally do it."

"So, let's see," Don said, "Your feet hurting because you were 150 pounds overweight didn't do it. Losing your job didn't do it. Your feet hurting worse, and your knees hurting too because you were 200 pounds overweight didn't do it. You had to experience humiliation, like a turtle on its back, to finally do it."

"Do what?" Donna asked, "Make him hit bottom?"

"Make him able to see into his mirror of badness," Larry said.

"Make him able to hear God talking to him through his body aches and pains," Don said. "Make him realize he was on an unhealthy path and needed to change."

"Same thing," Larry said. "When a person can see clearly into their *Mirror of Badness*, they can examine their life objectively for the very first time. It becomes obvious, they need to change.

"For you Abe, it took falling on your ass to wake you up and shine the light on your sinful life. You were a preacher, but you didn't get it. You didn't realize you were a sinner and needed to change like almost everyone else."

"You're right Larry," Abe said. "In all my years with the church, I really only wanted to impress my father. When I was young, I wanted to be the best pastor's son, but I failed at that. When I got older, I wanted to be the best pastor and grow the biggest Church in San Jose, but it was only to impress my human father. I really wasn't a born-again believer. I was more like an actor."

"But now you admit it! Now you see!" Larry exclaimed with excitement. "We have another blind man seeing! I know it sounds strange, but you idolized your father similar to how I idolized my hot wife."

"And look how you've changed," Don said. "Except for starving yourself into a coma, I'd say you're a true success story."

"I think a lot of people at the top of the church can't see their own badness," Abe Seabrooke said, "and a lot of others are desperately trying to hide it. I didn't have an impressive conversion story to tell everyone, so I said what a lot of pastors with PhD's said. I said I found the Lord as a child. My conversion story was a lie."

"How could a child experience being bad enough to really get it at such a young age?" Larry asked. "I guess anything's possible with God, but I can't relate."

"Maybe that pastor with a PhD fell in love with a pretty girl from Bible study and became the world's best preacher to impress the girl," Fonu said.

"That makes a lot of sense," Don said.

"It would sure help if preachers preached a little more about how bad they've been," Larry said. "Even if it was admitting they became a star homophobic preacher because they were lusting after a pretty church girl with a homophobic father."

"They're afraid to admit they have original sin too," Fonu said. "Because then we wouldn't trust them with our money."

"And they're right about that," Larry said. "So, they continue telling their childhood conversion story. They continue toing the line."

"While driving people like us crazy," Don said. "Maybe they should try to explain why a gay person should listen to a heterosexual homophobic man with a Bible who claims to be an expert on everything gay?"

"Exactly Don," Gerry said. "I just love the way you think."

"Maybe God's funny plan all along was to see if all the Christian people could really learn to love and accept gay people?" Larry said, laughing a little. "And all the people who couldn't learn to love and accept gay people were the chaff."

"That would be funny," Don said.

"Maybe God makes people gay for exactly that reason," Fonu said.

"And all the hurtful homophobes would be the ones burning in hell for eternity?" Gerry asked.

"If you believe in eternal hell," Larry replied. "That's why I believe in reincarnation."

"Me too," Don said.

"Please let's not get sidetracked on reincarnation!" Fonu exclaimed. "Let Don explain the part of our theory about gays in heaven."

"Well, we wanted to understand what Jesus taught about loving others, even our enemies," Don said.

"That includes gay people," Fonu said, looking at Gerry with a frown on his face.

"So, we recalled experiences we knew were true," Don said. "Like the very nice neighbor boy who grew up to be a very loving, gay, married monogamous father."

"And the big pervert in the men's room wanking his sausage behind me," Fonu said, with a scowl on his face.

"Yes, we've all had experiences," Don said. "So, we took all our experiences we knew were true, and combined them with what we'd learned from the sacred teachings. It became obvious, just like there are two kinds of heterosexual people, gay people come in two flavors too, either predominantly loving or predominantly mean, selfish and/or perverted."

"There are more than two kinds of gay men," Gerry said. "You've got jocks, bears, wolves, otters, chubs and twinks to name a few."

"I'm not talking about their size or hairiness," Don said, annoyed and staring at Gerry directly. "I'm talking about their thoughts. Specifically, what are they thinking while they're doing it? Are they having loving thoughts, or perverted and dominating thoughts? What's in your heart Gerry?" Don said, tapping his chest with his index finger. "Because your thoughts follow your heart. Are they loving and caring thoughts? Or, are you just feeling good getting your rocks off."

"Me Don?" Gerry asked, putting a finger to his lips. "You want to know my thoughts while I'm doing it?"

"No, not particularly Gerry," Don said. "I'm just saying, things aren't always black and white. It may not always be good for a man to have sex with his wife, because it depends on his thoughts at the time. You see, the act of sexual intimacy should be far more than just an act."

"For a shrink, you don't listen too well," Donna said. "I want loving thoughts as part of a loving, committed, monogamous relationship."

"Exactly," Don said, looking deeply in Donna's eyes. He could feel her loving heart. He could easily see past the big, dark ring dangling off her nose and see how beautiful she was. He repeated the end of Donna's sentence, "A loving, committed, monogamous relationship, isn't that what we all want?"

"It's ironic that some pastors with PhD's are teaching the homophobic lie and confusing God's truth," Larry said. "With PhD's in theology, they should understand the depth of God's love applies to gay people too."

"They may have ninety-nine percent of their Bible under-standing right, but to the one percent, they're blind," Don said. "And this may seem harsh, but I think those pastors with PhD's are committing the only unforgivable sin accord-ing to Jesus. With their authority and their lofty church position, they're teaching something that isn't one hundred percent true and saying it is. They're blaspheming the Holy Spirit, like the Pharisees."

"You got it Don!" Larry exclaimed. "That's the best explanation of blaspheming the Holy Spirit I've ever heard. The only unforgivable sin is reserved for the leaders of the church, like the pharisees, those teaching Gods word. Therefore, heterosexual pastors should be very careful when teaching about gay people."

"Especially when answering the 'Is it possible' ques-tions," Don said. "Like, is it possible for two gay people to love each other how God intends married people to love each other? If they teach it's not possible, and they cause insanity, ultimately driving people away from God, then they' re guilty of the only unforgivable sin."

"Saying something not true, and then saying it's from the Holy Spirt," Fonu said. "That's bad, very bad."

"They should just say they don't have a good answer," Gerry said. "It's as easy as that, because they're not gay."

"That was me," Abe said. "My conversion story was a lie, and I was blaspheming the Holy Spirit. I was commit-ting the only unforgivable sin. I was preaching and teaching something that was not one hundred percent the truth and saying it was God's word.

"Now I see it so clearly," Abe said, putting his head down with his hand on his forehead. "Like in Matthew 12:24, when the Jewish pharisees lied and said Jesus cast out demons by the power of Satan. And in James 3:1, where it says teachers will be judged more harshly. Now, I feel like I understand everything." Abe started sweating. He didn't look too good.

"Don't worry Abe," Larry said. "It's only unforgivable if you can't admit you were wrong."

"Yes, for sure," Don said, putting his hand on Abe's shoulder and looking him in the eyes. Don's calm touch made Abe feel like everything was going to be okay. "You had your homophobic awakening, so you'll be fine. I'm certain of it."

"I never understood how any sin could be unforgivable," Abe said, "or what it meant to blaspheme the Holy Spirit. Now, I get it! The only unforgivable sin was reserved for the leaders, those in authority, like I was. Leaders who taught something that was wrong, and said it was God's truth. If I was God, I'd be pissed off too."

"Those Jewish Pharisees sure didn't have a clue to the wisdom Jesus was teaching," Larry said. "They must have thought: Love my enemy? Eat with unbelievers? Turn the other cheek? Heal on the Sabbath? Give charity in secret? Pray in private? How will all the people know how good and holy I am if I give charity in secret and pray in private? Those Pharisees sure didn't get it."

"Like the homophobic preachers today who just don't get it," Gerry said. "The one percent that is. Why do they have to be experts on everything, including everything gay?"

"Yea, my father was an expert on everything too," Fonu Ali said. "He knew his Quran by heart and prayed five times a day. He taught me not to question a thing he said and just be good. If he was alive today, he'd be an expert on everything gay too."

"Did you pray in public places with your father?" Donna asked.

"Yes, I had to," Fonu replied. "We prayed in parking lots, gas stations and on the side of the road. One day I'll never forget, was the day after a deadly terror attack. We prayed at the gas station. It was so embarrassing. After praying, my father went into the store, and an old lady came up to me and said, 'Read the *Sermon on the Mount* sonny.' Then, she quickly left."

"My father said Americans were prejudiced against Muslims, and that the terrorists weren't really Muslims, and that the United States had it coming to them anyway, because they stole our oil. Well, my father was wrong about a lot of things. So, after he got trampled to death during the Hajj, I started reading the Bible, and the *Sermon on the Mount* was where I started.

"All I can say is, if Muhammad had read the *Sermon on the Mount*, he wouldn't have included praying in public as one of the five pillars of Islam. Jesus specifically taught not to do this. Jesus taught us to pray in private, not for the world to see. Jesus taught the purpose of prayer was to communicate with God, not to impress our neighbors."

"I think we're all in violent agreement here," Don said. "Muslims following strict Islamic rules without thinking are just as bad as Christian fundamentalists following what they've been taught without thinking."

"Or laughing for that matter," Larry said, chuckling with a big smile.

"They don't get that God has an infinite sense of humor too," Don said. "Some of the funniest stuff in the Bible was directed at the fundamentalists of the time."

"I think a lot more people would read the Bible, if they knew there were funny parts too," Larry said.

"The first thing an unhappy Muslim should do," Fonu Ali said, "is admit the possibility the Hajj was inserted by humans. Then, they should read the *Sermon on the Mount*. Once they understand the *Sermon on the Mount*, they're guaranteed to have an awakening."

"Do you mean a homophobic awakening Fonu?" Gerry asked, very seriously.

"No Gerry! I don't mean a homophobic awakening," Fonu said, with exasperation. "Why does everything have to be about your flipping homoness?"

"It's my life," Gerry replied.

"I think the awakening Fonu's referring to," Don said, "is the awakening of a fundamentalist person, a fundamentalist Muslim in this case, to the possibility their perfect sacred book might be one percent wrong. Like, maybe the Hajj wasn't such a great idea from God after all.

"This initial awakening is only the first step for a hard-line Muslim, like Fonu was. Once they understand how important their thoughts are, once they grasp the idea of thought sin and the idea of loving their enemies, then they might have their homophobic awakening. But due to the degree some Muslims have been brainwashed into homophobia, it may take years for a Muslim like Fonu to have a true homophobic awakening."

"Do you think I'm gay Don?" Abe Seabrooke asked.

"No, why would you ask that?" Don replied.

"I'm a Baptist preacher who's preached from the hardwired hetero point of view. And, I admit, I've demonized gays."

"At least you admitted you were wrong," Donna said, in a supportive way.

"I guess you would've fit the profile," Don said. "Up until the point I saw you hugging my gay neighbor and announce your homophobic awakening to everyone. I never thought of you in a sexual way at all. I couldn't imagine it."

"I've been attracted to men my whole life," Abe Seabrooke said, for the first time in his life.

"My word! This is big!" Gerry exclaimed, slapping his thighs and then squeezing his hands between his knees.

Fonu was looking at Abe with a new disgusting look on his face. It was a look like someone was trying to pull out his tongue with a pair of pliers, and someone else was holding a pile of dog poop under his nose. "That's so gross," Fonu Ali said.

"My father made faces like you," Abe said. "And I grew up with his mean words too, and his rigid understanding of the Bible. My father's agonizing faces said everything. His faces showed how he felt, when the subject of gay anything came up. He didn't have to say a word. His faces said it all, ever since I was three, and I picked up my sister's baby doll.

"I had no problem believing in original sin," Abe said, getting a little emotional. "Because of the faces he made, I felt like I was sin itself. I held a very deep, dark secret, and I couldn't tell anyone else. I couldn't imagine what my father would do if he found out. He was already so verbally abusive. I was too frightened to say a thing. So, I over-ate and drank to feel better, and I got fat."

"Are you aware of the correlation between severe eating disorders and child sexual abuse?" Gerry asked. "Sex abuse can turn someone into an obese cripple or an anorexic skeleton, starving to death while having plenty to eat."

"I tried to be as asexual as possible," Abe said. "But as a teenager, I got aroused changing in the locker room. It was so embarrassing. So, I just quit sports and made up excuses not to take PE.

"How could anybody love me?" Abe said. "I felt like maybe I was evil or something. I wasn't attracted to women at all, but I had lots of girlfriends. My father was a Baptist preacher and a big football jock with a son who was popping boners in the locker room. The writing was on the wall, and he knew it, but he couldn't accept it. He couldn't accept me. Therefore, he accepted the insanity it caused me instead.

"I just wanted my father to be proud of me. So, I put every ounce of energy into memorizing the Bible. I worked hard on my preaching skills too, and I finally impressed my father a little, when I became one of the most successful homophobic, rigid as stone preachers in the state.

"The gay haters and big-time meat eaters, like my father, loved my sermons. I preached a hyper-masculine message to men who loved to eat meat, and the women cleaved to them. We had 'meat only' men's potlucks that were a huge success. The church supplied the grill, and all the men brought their favorite meat. The way I was brainwashed growing up, vegetarians, environmentalists and the gay friendly were the enemy."

"Environmentalists and vegetarians too?" Dave slowly asked.

"Yes, for some reason a lot of fundamentalists ridicule vegetarians too," Don said. "I think it's because of the Cain and Abel story. God preferred Abel's meat sacrifice over Cain's vegetables. So, Cain got jealous and killed Abel. Some people like to use this story as an excuse to ridicule vegetarians, have all meat potlucks and eat like pigs. Some people just don't get it."

"On the flip side, some rigid as stone vegans don't get it either," Donna said. "I went vegan for a while, until my menstrual cycle stopped. My body said no to that rigid as stone crap."

"I wonder how many vegans cheat?" Fonu said, rubbing his chin and thinking.

"Yes Dave, my words came down on vegetarians too," Abe said. "Vegetarians who were only trying to be really good and healthy by not killing animals and eating them. My words from the pulpit told the meat loving fundamentalists exactly what they wanted to hear."

"You confirmed their theory," Don said.

"You made the wrong seem right in their own eyes," Larry said.

"Some fundamentalists don't give a damn about climate change either," Fonu said. "They think we're in the end times now, so it doesn't matter."

"They argue it can't be proved to be caused by humans," Larry said.

"As their wife drives her tank around town," Don said. "How selfish is that? Why not work on reducing pollution anyway? That sounds like a good big goal doesn't it?"

"We need to save the rain forests too," Dave chimed in.

"Yes Dave," Don said. "And grow a lot of plants like you do to gobble up the CO_2."

"Let's just agree to work on reducing pollution," Fonu said, "rather than waiting until climate change has been conclusively proven to be caused by humans. And can we agree too much carbon dioxide is pollution too? And the same thing with radiation spilling into the ocean? Bloody hell! Talk about unforgivable sins."

"If the climate change deniers could just admit the possibility they might be one percent wrong," Don said. "We might get to work on changing from oil to hydrogen power and clean up our planet and have an ocean without radiation for the whales and fish to swim in. And we'd be one step closer to world peace."

"Let's get back to your father abusing you Abe," Gerry said. "How exactly were you abused? Physically? Verbally? Thexually?"

"Oh, come on now Gerry!" Don exclaimed. "Everybody wasn't sexually abused, and Abe isn't your patient."

"It's okay Don. I can talk about my stuff now," Abe Seabrooke said. "I examined my entire life in that hospital. Even in the coma, this little computer upstairs was working." Abe pointed up. "I dreamed of talking to you, Fonu, Dave and Gerry. I dreamed of all the conversations we had these past few years.

"Then, when I came out of the coma, I kept thinking about you guys. I kept hearing you inside my mind talking about your theories, and then I had my awakening. I concluded that you and Fonu were right. My church and I were teaching something that was at least one percent in error, because we looked at people only one way, the gender binary or hardwired heterosexual way. I demonized gay people, and I couldn't even accept myself. I was so screwed up, and I was wrong, because God makes people like me too, hardwired gay. Therefore, when the Bible is interpreted and taught from only the hardwired heterosexual perspective, it sounds insane to a hardwired homosexual person. It's so obvious to me now. If the interpretation sounds insane to someone, then something's wrong with the message somewhere."

"Yes," Gerry said. "It's presumptuous to conclude that people who disagree with you are mentally ill or demon possessed, just because you can't relate to having loving feelings for someone of the same sex."

"I asked myself, how would the gospel sound to Gerry coming from me?" Abe said, looking at Gerry. "And then I broke down crying. I felt so bad. I cried, and I cried for I don't know how long. And then it was like, suddenly I understood everything. Like Larry said, I finally saw clearly into my *Mirror of Badness*. I was a gay homophobic preacher.

"My preaching drove people away from God's love. Somehow, I made the good news sound bad to gay people and people who loved gay people. People who knew God made people very different. I caused people to fall away from belief in miracles, give up on the supernatural and have to come up with their own stupid ass theories. So far, I've spent half my life driving people away from God. Now, I see clearly. People should be taught *The Insertion Theory* too, along with God's story of love. If not, the message can get distorted into the fundamentalist message I was teaching.

"Then it hit me, like a yes message from God," Abe said enthusiastically. "Like Don says, anyone who has a problem with organized religion should go to *Church in the Park*, with no holy middlemen. Once millions of people start going to the park Sunday morning, the Pope might think twice about church doctrine.

"I was blind and rigid as stone. Then, I saw clearly. I didn't get it, but all of a sudden I did. I used to think all the gay accepting people were deceived by Satan or had a demon in them. Then I realized, I was the brainwashed one. And like Don says, we need to get re-brainwashed with love if we want world peace. Well, in that hospital, somewhere between life and death, all our conversations were going through my head."

"So, what was it?" Don asked. "What was it that finally turned the light on and helped things make sense. We had lots of conversations."

"Well," Abe said, pausing and getting a little emotional again. "I saw Gerry as a young boy, and I heard his father telling him that Jesus didn't love girly boys. And I cried, because that was me. And I couldn't stop thinking about the effing machines, and the two naked guys, and the thoughts going through their heads. The conclusion I had was, loving thoughts and being truthful were what mattered most.

"It was then, I had my homophobic awakening like you guys are always talking about. And I knew I had to come out of the closet too. I realized, it wasn't being gay that mattered, it was being honest and having loving thoughts."

"It sounds like a documented homophobic awakening to me," Don said. "Abe finally broke through his brainwashing. All it took was good communicating."

Don smiled. He felt like he'd just achieved one of his big goals in life. He looked around the room proudly. Abe was like Don's very large, gay and gay accepting, baby. "All we did was talk about the problems that arise when literally interpreting anything, other than mathematics.

We talked about how one's perfect interpretation of the Bible couldn't be perfect when applied to someone else who was different."

CHAPTER 25

Church in the park

"Abe Seabrooke got it!" Don exclaimed, as he clapped his hands once and went over to high five Fonu Ali. "Can you believe it Fonu! In this corner we have," Don said it like a ring announcer at a boxing match, "formerly the fattest fundamentalist in town, who has lost over one hundred pounds, introducing the new senior coordinator of *Church in the Park*, San Jose, with a salary of zero, Abraham Seabrooke."

Everyone started clapping, as Abe blushed and emotionally said, "Stop kidding around Don."

"I'd dub you senior pastor, but the title sounds too holy," Don said with a big smile. "Who's kidding Abe? But if you think people having *Church in the Park* is a joke…"

"No, I don't Don!" Abe said assertively. "I love you guys and your theory and our cult and the *Church in the Park* idea, but are you serious? Can we really do it?" Then Abe remembered another dream he had. He pointed to the ceiling as he recalled this amazing dream.

"I had this dream Don. It was so real. It was like I had died, and I was on my way to heaven. I was in the arms of Jesus, flying up into the stratosphere. I felt warm and loved, and I understood I was loved completely. I heard no words, but I understood, I could come home now, or remain on Earth for the important work that needed doing.

"I clearly understood I couldn't be loved any more for doing the important work, because I was already loved completely. I said yes in my thoughts. Yes, I wanted to go back and do the important work, and then I woke up.

"I came out of my coma, but I didn't know what the important work was I was supposed to do. Now I know Don! It's *Church in the Park*, don't you see? This is huge. But I have no idea where to start. We're talking about changing the world here. It seems too big for me."

"That was a near-death dream!" Don exclaimed. "And near-death dreams got to be listened to!" Don was thinking deeply about Abe's dream. Then he started thinking about world peace.

"In the arms of Jesus, being told how much God loves you," Larry said, "that's deep. And the understanding that your works aren't the reason why, but important work will be the result."

"It'll be a step towards world peace," Don said. "It's spiritual evolution, don't you see? Once the pope hears about all the people going to the park Sunday mornings, once the Holy See sees, maybe he'll listen to us. And that'll be the beginning of real communication and real change."

"You should re-read Exodus in the Bible," Larry said, looking at Abe. "The part where God told Moses to go to Pharaoh and lead the Jews out of Egypt. Moses replied, 'Who am I to go to Pharaoh?' Moses had the same insecurities you're expressing Abe, but God told him not to worry, because he'd be with him."

"Of course, *Church in the Park* will be a big challenge. We love big challenges," Don said, with a big smile and a twinkle in his eyes. "I know Fonu and Dave will help out. What about you Larry, in between rescues or something?"

"Sure thing Don, I'm in," Larry said. "Taking on organized religion sounds just crazy enough for me. Please just promise me this isn't some new cult you're starting."

"By definition, it can't be a cult if we don't accept money," Don said. "And money causes problems anyway, so we won't accept money. We'll preach love your enemy and love your neighbor directly, without holy middlemen, like Abe said."

"Let's start in downtown San Jose, smack dab in the middle of Saint James Park," Abe said. "The first *Church in the Park* for people who've had it with organized religion."

"Are you serious Don?" Donna asked, with a questioning look on her face. "Start a church? A *Church in the Park*?"

"The church at large has problems, doesn't it?" Don asked. "I'm sure there's something you'd like to change about organized religion."

"Yes," Donna replied. "Everyone does."

"I refuse to give my money to pay for sex pervert lawsuits," Fonu said with a grimace.

"Same here," Larry said. "The problem is having church employees dubbed holy when they're not, combined with a large organization's deep pockets full of money."

"Agreed," Don said. "So, *Church in the Park* won't accept money, and it won't have employees with titles that sound holy. We'll have no pastors, priests, deacons or elders or buildings with secret rooms. Therefore, *Church in the Park* will have no payoffs, coverups, lawsuits or sex abuse."

"That sounds like a good idea to me," Fonu said.

"Everyone has a story about something they dislike about organized religion," Don said. "That's why so many people are falling away from the church and our culture is throwing out everything sacred. Therefore, something needs to change, because we're missing out on good things too. Somebody definitely needs to start something. Why not us! I'm for damn sure serious!"

"We'll have to go on a float soon," Fonu said. "I have some questions to drop into the silence about *Church in the Park*. Like, how do you help a filthy, drunk, belligerent homeless person who doesn't want help, that is, if it means giving up drinking or drugs?"

"That's a tough one," Don said. "Nobody wants to bring home a filthy drunken stranger."

"Give 'em good socks," Dave said.

"That would be a start," Don said. "Good idea Dave. We could give 'em good socks with *Church in the Park* written across the top. Those four words might start the conversation needed to solve a drunk guy's problem. We definitely need to make a list and go on a float. Donna, would you like to try exploring the great beyond and go floating? Maybe drop some questions into the meditation silence? Like, how does one start a *Church in the Park* that brings love and sanity to everyone?"

"I'm not sure I could get into starting a church," Donna said. "How I grew up, you know, I'm kind of turned off to Church and the whole, God He thing."

"Either way, it's good to talk about it," Don said. "Look, we're not trying to brainwash you into another God He cult church like you've experienced. One of our big goals is to un-brainwash people."

"Including ourselves," Fonu Ali said.

"Why do you think so many Americans get fat?" Don asked.

"Because we're brainwashed to eat crap," Abe answered automatically.

"You see, Abe got re-brainwashed with love," Don said. "Love for the truth, love for others who are different, love for his body temple, and of course, love for carrots, apples, beets and cabbage. It's important to note, to be successfully re-brainwashed, one must be un-brainwashed first."

"The word, 'church' is problematic for a lot of us," Gerry said, with quotes in the air. "We associate that word with religious people who whisper, look askance at us and sometimes say mean things. Maybe we should call it the loving gathering in the park."

Fonu's face twisted as he said, "How will people know we're having church, if we don't call it church? We need to call it church."

188 | DAVID DEWAR ROBERTS

"Don't think of it as church then Gerry," Don said. "Think of it as graduate school for the supernatural part of you. And look, even if you don't believe in miracles, think of it as getting to know your neighbors. *Church in the Park* might help break the ice with our heavy accented neighbors. *Church in the Park* can help in a lot of ways. It's always good to get to know your neighbors."

"Maybe it'll help some foreigners get rid of their heavy friggin' accents," Fonu said, with a scowl. "I get such a headache trying to understand what they're saying."

"Come on Fonu, that's so trivial it's not worth mentioning," Don said. "And with your tone and the faces you make, you come off like you're prejudiced against foreigners, and you're Tongan and Afghani. *Church in the Park* will be about getting together with our neighbors and giving thanks to our creator. We'll sing and share our different experiences, that led to how we now believe. We'll share all the different ways we can love our neighbors. It won't be about complaining about their heavy accents Fonu."

"Sorry Don," Fonu said. "We could bring sandwiches for people who are hungry, to go with their socks."

"You better let Dave carry the sandwiches Fonu," Gerry said. "Sounds like you're still obsessed."

Fonu made a face, with his lips pushed out.

"Bringing sandwiches for people who are hungry is a great idea," Don said. "*Church in the Park* will be a fun social experiment too. And with Abe Seabrooke as our senior coordinator in San Jose, how can we lose? Abe will be our walking talking openly gay weight loss success story. Maybe some fat homophobes from Abe's old church will see his weight loss and start questioning some things they were taught. And we'll seek the whole truth, not just the truth that caters to me or you. And we won't accept money."

"Because money is at the root of all Church problems," Larry interjected. "It's so obvious to me. Anyone else?"

"Me too," Donna said. "Because money equals power."

"Totally obvious," Don said. "We got to eliminate money from the equation."

"Yup," Fonu said.

"Agreed," Abe said.

"You can call it what you want," Don said. "It will be a loving gathering unlike any church because it doesn't cause insanity for gay people or ask for your money."

"That doesn't sound like church to me," Donna said. "Which is good!"

"I know!" Don exclaimed. "It's unheard of! Soon, all the closeted Christians, or people who can't accept the Christian label, will be coming out to their local park in droves. We'll be sending a strong message to the Pope. A message that says, if you don't have a good answer just say so!

"And, instead of giving money to a Church with employees and salaries, small groups of people can band together and love their neighbors directly and anonymously, saying it's from *Church in the Park*," Don said. "If people need help..."

"They can go to the park," Larry said, completing Don's sentence. "I think it's perfect. If there's an earthquake and people need help, they can go to the park. If people want to give thanks to God, they can go to the park. If people want to help others…"

Then everyone said in unison, "They can go to the park."

"I think *Church in the Park* in the rain would be cool," Dave said, as he began to sing.

DAVE'S SONG FOR CHURCH IN THE PARK IN THE RAIN

"Put on your boots and grab your umbrella
and come out to the park and sing
Rain or shine we gather together
and give thanks to our King."
"Or Queen," Gerry chimed in.

"We get up early and go out to the park
and give thanks for our dreams
We hug each other and pray together
With gratitude for our King,

"Give thanks, give thanks, give thanks and love your neighbor
Try to understand them if they're different than you
Yes, love them, especially if they're different
You gotta really love your neighbor
Not just pray for them to be like you

"So, grab your neighbor and come out to the park
come out to the park and sing
give thanks and hugs and dance together
And praise our loving King

Amen, amen, that we are all together
Give thanks, give thanks, give thanks and love your neighbor
Try to understand living in their shoes
You gotta really love your neighbor
Not just pray for them to be like you.

DAVE HETFIELD—2031

"Dave sang a song at full speed!" Don exclaimed. "Dave hasn't sung a note since his partial lobotomy ten years ago, and now he just belted out a new song at full speed. It's an affirmation for *Church in the Park*! I think we just witnessed a healing!"

"Nice song Dave, but I thought you were an atheist," Fonu said.

"I am, but *Church in the Park* sounds fun, with lots of hugs," Dave said, at slow speed again.

"Absolutely, lots of hugs," Abe Seabrooke said. "That's another thing I brought back from my dreams. Somehow, I remember, it takes seven hugs to overcome one hurtful word. So, as senior coordinator of *Church in the Park*, San Jose, I vote in favor of lots of hugs."

"Don?" Gerry asked. "When you say all the closeted Christians like us will be coming out in droves... do you mean you're...?"

"No Gerry! Sorry!" Don said. "I use the term 'closeted Christian' to define what I think is a huge majority of people in the world. People who dislike the politics of organized religion. People who believe in what Jesus taught, but who have been turned off to the Christian label. People who refuse to give their hard-earned money to rigid as stone fundamentalists with microphones, or to pay for sex perverts lawsuits."

"I'm a closeted Christian then," Gerry said.

"Me too," Donna said.

CHAPTER 26

In the Wild You'd Be Dead

"So, Abe," Gerry said, as he crossed his legs like a woman and stroked his goatee. "I'm happy to hear about your awakening. It must have been oh so hard, so very, very hard growing up gay with a homophobic preacher for a father. I can relate. My father wasn't a preacher, but he used the Bible as a weapon too, and that's abuse enough for gay people like us."

"It was mostly verbal," Abe said. "No broken bones or concussions. I got the belt now and then. You know, spare the rod spoil the child. It was really no big deal. It seemed like a normal childhood to me."

"All childhoods seem normal when you're a child Abe," Gerry said, in a thoughtful, caring way. "Talking about it always helps. Talking can help us remember and remembering can help us deal with it and heal. Don't forget what Don said, if you keep your words in…"

"You'll never get the weight off," Abe responded automatically.

"So, you said the abuse was mostly physical and verbal? What about the sexual? Are you sure you weren't abused sexually?" Gerry pressed, as Don was getting visibly irritated by Gerry's aggressive questioning.

"It's okay Don, I don't mind talking about it. Maybe there's something about dying and coming back to life that changes people. Now, I can talk about my stuff, because I really don't care what people think anymore. It's like I'm beyond that now. It's like I'm on a different plain, free and way out there," Abe said, as he stretched his out arms in front of him and then to the sides, like he was calling someone safe at home plate in slow motion.

"Gerry likes to push people to the limit sometimes," Don said.

"Oh, does he now? I never noticed," Fonu said sarcastically, making one of his faces.

"I also had a step uncle who was a pervert, but I suppressed it for years," Abe said.

"Oh, my poor baby, let it out, let it out," Gerry said, like a mama bear wanting to help her cub.

"It all came back to me in the hospital," Abe said. "I had so many amazing dreams in the coma, but this one was a nightmare. I saw a man looking at me with a very strange look in his eyes. Then he kissed me deeply, and I pushed him away with all my might. I felt his whiskers, and I smelled something very familiar. It was the smell of my step uncle. Then suddenly, I remembered everything."

"What exactly did he do?" Gerry asked.

"Well, he liked to horse around a lot," Abe said. "At least that's what he called it. I recall it being like a game at the time, up until the point he kissed me deeply. That's when I freaked out and fought him off like a wildcat. I don't think it ever happened again. It was really no big deal."

"I'll be the judge of that," Gerry said. "Oh, you poor baby, just let it out, let it out. How old were you and exactly what was going on right before your step uncle kissed you?"

"I was very young at the time," Abe said, "maybe five or six, and my step uncle used to baby-sit us. He really liked us kids, or me, I guess. He didn't play as much with my sisters. My dream helped me remember. He liked to tickle and wrestle with me and horse around especially before my bath. I remembered in the dream, as we were wrestling, I felt rubbing between my thighs."

"Oh my," Gerry said with a finger to his lips. "Were your clothes on, or were you naked during the wrestling?"

"I was naked," Abe said. "It was before my bath."

"Your step-uncle wrestled with you naked and rubbed between your thighs?" Gerry said with his eyes wide open. "The technical term is intercural and that most definitely was child sexual abuse."

"I guess so," Abe said. "I didn't realize it at the time, until he kissed me. I knew that was bad. That kiss was so gross. It still creeps me out just thinking about it. I'll never forget the look he had. He had the strangest look in his eyes."

"Intercural?" Larry asked, looking at Gerry seriously.

"It means between the thighs," Gerry explained. "Like some Greek soldiers did with boys in the military."

Gerry looked at Abe very seriously and said, "Of course he had a strange look in his eyes. He was looking at you like a sexual object. That look affected your entire life. That look was the reason you gained so much weight. You see, when you're fat, people won't look at you like that. So, in a sick way, your fat makes you feel safe, but that's a lie because being fat is not good for you or safe."

Everyone was feeling a little uncomfortable with Abe's revelation. "That look came from a demon inside your step uncle," Larry said.

"Being fat is definitely not good for you," Fonu said. "Just think if you had to run away from a terrorist. I think about it all the time. I couldn't do it. I'm too fat. Have you ever noticed how thin the terrorists are? They're all so skinny. I notice it all the time."

"The Buddha nearly starved himself to death," Don said. "Then he changed paths. He realized starvation wasn't where it's at."

"The terrorists are just trying to prove to the world how good they are," Larry said. "Since overeating is bad, starving yourself must be good right? And since Muslims don't believe Jesus died for the original sin inside of them, they need to be really, really good to balance out all their bad. Same with pagans and atheists."

"And Jews and Hindus," Fonu said.

"The skinny young terrorists probably fast every day," Don said. "That's what Muhammad taught in the Hadith. If a young man is horny and can't afford a few wives, he should avoid eating. After a few days, the urges will go away."

"Brilliant advice!" Fonu Ali exclaimed, shaking his head. "And then for their final good deed, they can blow themselves up in a crowded place full of people who believe in freedom, like us."

"You got to appreciate the brainwashing there," Don said. "And yes Fonu, in the wild you'd be dead."

CHAPTER 27

Protecting Our Kids

"Your step uncle thighed you? That's friggin' evil," Donna said.

"He could've kept on thighing me as far as I was concerned. I was so young, I didn't even realize it was abuse until the kiss," Abe said. "It wasn't that bad, only thighing and a kiss."

"Only thighing and a kiss!" Gerry exclaimed, slapping his knees. "Look, it doesn't take orifice penetration to screw up an innocent child. You poor baby! Your step uncle used you for sex and that should not happen! Children need to be protected!" Gerry sobbed a little, then he took a deep breath and very seriously said, "Maybe consciously, you didn't know it was abuse until the kiss, but subconsciously, I guarantee you, it was abuse, and it screwed you up!"

"You're such a drama queen Gerry," Fonu said. "Everyone goes through crap. We all get tested. Some of us just get a more effed up test, that's life."

"It made you who you are today," Don said. "Senior Coordinator of *Church in the Park*, San Jose."

"Children need to be protected!" Donna said forcefully. "Don't minimize what he's been through Fonu. That's like heaping more abuse on top of abuse."

"I feel his pain," Gerry said, still sobbing.

"Maybe getting thighed as a child is what turned you guys gay," Fonu said.

"Fonu! That's like saying God doesn't make people gay," Don said. "And we both know same sex attraction is a lot more complicated than that." Then Don exclaimed, "I got it! Another big goal for *Church in the Park*!

"We all want to protect children from pedophiles, right?" Everybody nodded. "And we've all heard fundamentalists who demonize gay people and say they're all pedophiles who want to turn our kids gay?" Everybody nodded again. "Well, at *Church in the Park* we'll gather statistics about people who molest children and look at the data for ourselves. We'll do the work and find out for ourselves.

"We'll encourage gay activists and religious fundamentalists to stop fighting each other and work proactively together fighting the pedophiles and the organizations that mislead us. I predict the data will show that most gay people aren't child molesters who want to turn our children gay. Then, we'll expose the lie some religious organizations have been spreading.

"And everyone will be encouraged to share their story, even gay activists and Muslim fundamentalists..."

"Wait, wait, wait," Abe interrupted. "You're suggesting right-wing homophobes work with gay activists?" Abe was thinking hard. "And you want to let Muslims have the microphone?"

"Yes Abe," Don said. "Communication with people who are very different is very good. And communication must be a two-way street."

"Okay, I like the idea of gays working with fundamentalists to protect the children," Abe said. "It sounds just crazy enough to be a really good idea. But giving Muslims the microphone at *Church in the Park* is something I must disagree with."

"I dubbed you senior coordinator Abe, but I'm the Grand Mufti. I'm the one you come to for answers," Don said, smiling and looking at Abe deeply. Don had a unique look of confidence when he had a truly good idea, like the confidence one gets playing poker with a high straight flush or playing chess when you can think eight moves ahead. Don's incredible brain could think like this, and he just knew communication held the answer to world peace. Therefore, Don was very confident. He looked at Abe and Abe capitulated.

"Of course, Don. You're the Grand Mufti," Abe said.

Don continued, "Of course the Muslims. Especially the Muslims! What the Muslim people believe is what every non-Muslim person should be studying nowadays. People who haven't studied the Quran want to open our borders to all Muslim countries. While the people who've done their homework say watch out, because Islam wants to kill our freedoms.

"I've studied the Quran and the Hadith. So, I'd love to hear the Muslim woman down the street explain the joyful, loving place she's at. I would love to hear her tell of the peace of Islam, when the Quran teaches people to think bad thoughts of others who believe differently, and others who don't believe at all.

"One thing I'm certain of," Don said, looking around the circle directly at each person, "thinking bad thoughts of others is bad. The Buddha taught, we must be mindful of our thoughts."

"That's what Jesus taught too," Larry interjected. "Even our bad thoughts are bad."

"Yes, because bad thoughts lead to offensive words and offensive words stop communication!" Don said emphatically. "And we need to communicate if we really want world peace! Our thoughts are what it's all about man!" Don exclaimed. "Specifically, I'd like to hear my Muslim neighbor explain why, in the case of accidental death, a Jewish, Christian or unbelieving person's life is only worth one third that of a Muslim's. Or, why is a Muslim woman's testimony only worth one half that of a Muslim man's?"

"That's totally old testament thinking!" Larry exclaimed, looking at Don. "Like what, now the Muslims are the chosen ones, and the Jews, atheists and Christians are unclean partial people?"

"I know," Don said. "That's why my new theory is the Quran was written by Jewish lawyers. Either way, I'd like to hear my Muslim neighbor explain their feelings about people who are different."

"What?" Fonu asked, looking at Don intensely with a new scrunched up look on his face. "You think the Quran was written by Jewish lawyers? You never told me that."

"Can you agree Muhammad had a point?" Don asked.

"I guess, about some catholic stuff, but I was born a Muslim and I know the Quran," Fonu said. "The Quran teaches Muslims to rule the world with a sword, willingly submit and not complain about freedoms being taken away."

"Not complain about freedoms being taken away?" Donna asked. "That sounds un-American to me, but I must admit, I've never read the Quran. I know nothing about Islam except the murders, burkas, bombings and shootings."

"It sounds like you have some reading to do," Don said. "Historically, leaders have tried to brainwash their people into believing the enemy was sub-human. Therefore, people could slaughter other people without a thought, because they thought of them as sub-human. This was a lie, of course, because all the dead people were indeed human. That's what comes to mind when I think of the Old Testament and the Quran."

"Hitler brainwashed the German people to murder millions of their Jewish neighbors," Fonu said. "He convinced the German people to believe the lie that the Jews were sub-human. Talk about smart people doing stupid freeking things."

"Don't forget the Nazis killed gay people too," Gerry said. "As well as Slavs, Poles, gypsies and Jehovah's witnesses."

"And disabled people," Dave said slowly.

"And like in America," Donna said. "People were brainwashed to believe the native people were less than human. So, the brainwashed people attempted to slaughter an entire culture, while the people doing the slaughtering thought they were such friggin' good Christians."

"And don't forget the Africans and the Chinese," Gerry said. "Americans were brainwashed to believe we were less than human too. Therefore, slavery, murder, rape and overall injustice could occur for generations, while the slave owners still thought they were oh so good, because they only raped the humans they owned. They loved their laws written in stone."

"Therefore, we all need to examine how we were brainwashed growing up," Don said. "And if there's a book, a pope, a pastor or an imam causing us to think less of others, that's bad. So, we all need to be mindful of our thoughts. And if we're thinking bad thoughts of others, we need to ask ourselves why. We don't need to kill people for it to be bad.

"Some things I read in the Quran would inspire bad thoughts toward anyone who wasn't a Muslim, similar to how the old testament would inspire bad thought towards anyone who wasn't a Jew. And bad thoughts are not what God wants. Bad thoughts are as bad as bad actions, because that's where they lead. It may only be a curled-up lip or a scrunched-up face," Don said, looking at Fonu intensely.

"That's why Muslims and Jews need to read what Jesus taught in the new testament," Larry said.

"So yes, I'd love to hear my Muslim neighbor explain their feelings, and tell me why they believe how they believe,"

Don said. "And I'd love to hear what their good big goal was too. But, if they're thinking bad thoughts about my neighbor because he's Jewish, Christian, atheist or gay, or if their supposedly good big goal is taking our freedoms away, then I'd say that's not a good big goal. That's a bad big goal, and there's a big difference."

"It's thsooo big," Gerry lisped, as he put his hands together wanting attention.

"What's so big now?" Fonu asked, looking at Gerry with a scowl.

"The difference," Gerry said. "The difference between a good big goal and a bad big goal. If one's big goal is family honor more than the truth, then that's not good. I know. I've counseled many gay Arabic men with severely homophobic fathers. One committed suicide, and several others feared for their lives. They wouldn't dare come out of their closet and stop living their lie. It's funny, all the religions say they have the truth, but if a gay person must live a lie to be accepted by their church, or to be loved by their father...."

"Then there must be something at least one percent wrong somewhere," Donna interjected.

"It's like people are being brainwashed to have bad thoughts towards gay people," Gerry said, looking over at Fonu. "And that's bad."

"We all suffer from some sort of brainwashing," Larry said. "And we need to realize this before we can get better. It's too bad some people don't want to get better. At least that's how it seems to me."

"And it's too bad," Fonu said, "in some countries, if you want to change and get better you might get killed by your own family members. In Afghanistan, don't even think about discussing the *Sermon on the Mount*. Pretty much, if you want to change and get better, they will kill you."

"Your story means a lot to me Fonu," Don said. "I'd still like to hear from my Muslim neighbor."

CHAPTER 28

The Smartest People Do the Stupidest Things

"Yes, some countries outlaw the Bible," Larry said. "In America, we just stigmatize people who believe it. A lot of truly Jewish people believe the Old Testament Bible was supernatural, they just don't believe Jesus was the Messiah. A lot of truly Muslim people believe Jesus was a prophet born of a virgin named Mary, and they believe the Quran was supernatural. They just don't believe Jesus died on the cross.

"And wars have been fought, and people continue to be killed because of these different peoples beliefs. What's a trip is, the Bible and the Quran contend to tell the same story and have a lot of the same characters..."

"And everyone's arguing about the end of story!" Don interjected excitedly. "That's why we can't have world peace!"

"Exactly Don!" Larry confirmed. "Meanwhile, many well educated, peace-loving people know nothing about these books or the supernatural."

"Tell everyone your theory Larry," Don said. "You know about the shamans reading the stars."

"Okay, well, one thing the Christian, Muslim and Jewish believers all agree on is the supernatural origin of the book of Psalms," Larry said. "And Psalms 19 says God's story was written in the stars when the universe was formed. Well, today everyone's arguing about the end of the story.

"My theory is, a million years before people started writing down these messages in the stars, people were much smarter than they are today. In ancient times people were more like shamans. They were less contaminated, and they had incredible vision. So, they could read God's Story written in the stars directly.

"These ancient shaman-like people interpreted the stars differently, like humans tend to do. They told many, many stories with a lot of the same basic themes, like be good, think of others, work hard and don't have sex with your sister, and a lot of other really good advice.

"These stories were passed down orally for millennia until people were so polluted they lost their shamanic qualities. People couldn't read the stories in the stars anymore, but around this same time, some of the smartest people learned how to read and write.

"And then later, God's Story came to life with characters like Noah and Abraham. Then Moses was born to lead the Jews out of Egypt. These characters lived lives that became many amazing stories, which other people wrote down later. These stories became the foundation of the three monotheistic religions of the world."

"What about Buddhism and Hinduism?" Dave asked.

"Buddhist, Hindu and native people's holy stories were in the stars too. They were all part of the big story, but Hinduism isn't monotheistic," Larry said. "And a Buddhist can be a Christian or an atheist, so it gets complicated."

"The Bhagavat Gita can make an atheist believe in God," Don said.

"Don't get Larry sidetracked Dave!" Fonu Ali exclaimed, with a serious scrunched up look on his face. "I like how he explains it! Please, let's not drift off and start arguing about reincarnation or if Buddhists are atheist! I'll get a headache!"

"Sorry," Dave said, moving a finger across his lips.

Larry continued, "Well, the ancient Jewish people were writing down some of the most incredible stories and prophetic messages. And they were a God-fearing people, so the writers and editors were being as honest and objective as humans could possibly be. The thing that changed everything was, some of the messages started coming true.

"These prophetic writings were labelled sacred, and the writers were called prophets, as long everything they predicted came true. If a single thing didn't come true, the prophet label was removed, and the false prophet was run out of town if he was lucky, but most likely he was stoned to death.

"At first, the scriptures were hard to understand, but after things started coming true, it was obvious something supernatural was going on. It wasn't long before the Jewish people believed and became very interested in these writings, which became the Bible's Old Testament. And they'd pay good money to hear these messages too. So, like a perfect plan, the people controlling the sacred scripture became the leaders of the Jewish people.

"Then, when Jesus died on the cross, and was pierced, and had no broken bones, and they gambled for his clothes, and they couldn't find his body three days later, the ending of the whole story became apparent. The Messiah was a lamb not a lion. Now, the entire thousand plus page string of messages written down over several centuries made sense. The super smart Jewish leaders in charge of God's sacred messages realized they had requested the crucifixion of their own savior. Like it was written in Isaiah 29:14, God frustrated the intelligence of the intelligent."

"Sometimes the smartest people do the stupidest things," Don said.

"Yes, but the saddest thing was, they couldn't admit it!" Larry said. "The Jewish leaders couldn't admit they did something so bad and accept God's loving forgiveness, because their pride was in the way. They were embarrassed. They were really, really smart, and what they did was really, really wrong. They knew they'd lose their standing in the community too, and their great job running the Jewish religion. They knew they'd lose everything. They were the Jewish police, and they were the smartest and most well-educated people on the planet. They knew all the rules. In the New Testament, they were called the Pharisees.

"So, the Jewish people who knew they needed forgiveness, became followers of what Jesus taught. While the Jewish leaders, the ones on top, refused to admit they needed forgiveness. They denied what they did and chose to spread insanity instead. Like it says in Isaiah 9:16, 'Those on the top, who guide this people, mislead them.'

"So, the followers of what Jesus taught were re-labeled Christians. The Christians assumed command of what was originally the Jewish religion. Now, the Christians were in control of publishing the sacred scripture. It was planet Earth's newest religion, soon to become another huge money-making venture. Now, the Catholic Church was in charge. The baton had been passed, and still, the Jewish leaders at the top wouldn't admit their error. They were still too prideful to see their badness in the mirror."

Larry was talking like a shaman and everyone understood everything very clearly.

"It didn't take long for the humans running the Catholic Church to start causing problems with the people. Especially in Arabia, where a lot of men were grumbling about the way the Catholics were running things, similar to the way the Jews out in the wilderness were always grumbling about the way Moses was running things. Now, the Arab men were the ones grumbling about the Catholics. These grumbling Arabs were probably the first to define themselves as spiritual but not religious, because they wanted several wives, but the Catholics said that was bad. You know, we humans will always grumble as long as another human is in charge, but Jesus taught we could have God in charge instead."

"That's radical," Donna said. "You are on a mission from God. I never heard the Bible explained that way. You are incredible Mr. Larry Cooley."

"That's why we need *Church in the Park*," Fonu said. "So we can have God in charge instead."

"Sounds like we're back to simplifying the problem by eliminating humans from the equation," Don said.

"Like how the effing machine question can help someone understand the whole gay thing?" Gerry asked, in a deadly serious manner.

"It's similar Gerry," Don said. "But Larry's talking about eliminating humans at the top of the church organization. The know-it-alls-who-don't-know-it-all at the top are always the problem, because they can't admit the possibility they might be one percent wrong about anything."

"Yes," Larry said. "Like the Jewish people in charge at the time couldn't accept what Jesus taught. And then, five hundred years later, the Arabic men couldn't accept the way the Catholics were running things. And then, a thousand years later, Martin Luther couldn't accept the way the Catholics were running things either, because he already had six kids, and he wanted to start pulling out to prevent conception, but the pope said that was bad.

"You see, Martin Luther had a very sexy wife who was fertile as a mouse. It seemed to him his sperm were swimming for at least a week in her. Natural family planning just wasn't working for the Luther family, and they had a big goal to accomplish. And they were a team. They just couldn't handle any more kids. So, up sprang the Lutherans.

"And then, a lot of grumbling men, who didn't like the way the Lutherans were running things, started listening to John Calvin. These men weren't very good at pulling out in time, and they were a little kinky too. They wanted to have sex in different ways to prevent conception. And so, up sprang the Calvinists. The Calvinists you see, were the first pro-anal Christians."

"Really? That's fascinating," Gerry said. "I never would have guessed it. From my experience with Calvinists, they seem the most homophobic. And they're pro-anal? It just doesn't make sense."

"I think it makes perfect sense," Don said, "because anal sex is what comes to mind when the topic of gay acceptance comes up, at least for us guys. The Calvinists, who like anal sex, don't want to be compared with two men doing the same thing. Therefore, today's Calvinists are the most homophobic of all. They're trying their best to have one hundred percent loving thoughts, and not think of sodomy, while they're practicing their favorite form of birth control."

"And we'll never know the Calvinist's thoughts while they're doing it," Fonu said.

"And the Calvinist will never know the gay persons thoughts while they're doing it," Don said. "Therefore, at some point, we need to leave it up to God."

"It's so hypocritical," Larry said. "That's why compassionate people are staying away from church. We're getting bombed, shot and run over by Muslim terrorists on one hand, and our gay children are getting bullied by Calvinists and Catholics on the other. Therefore, a lot of compassionate, well educated people are remaining on the sidelines with the Buddhists, patting their ears and humming with no need to hear about miracles or the Bible, because religions and religious people, they have concluded, were the problem in the world.

"So, many super smart people have absolutely zero interest in the supernatural. They know nothing about what the Jewish prophets started writing down thousands of years ago. They were taught, all through public school, that studying these ancient Jewish writings was just a waste of time."

"A lot of people think meditation's a waste of time too," Don said.

"I know, studying math, computers and physics seems so much more practical," Fonu said. "Therefore, many highly educated people know nothing about these books or the supernatural."

"A lot of very smart people have thrown out the sacred writings," Larry said. "But I wager they have a pretty good theory. That's why I like your *Insertion Theory*, because it includes the ancient messages about God. It's so much easier to come up with a theory that rejects the Bible and everything sacred. It's so much easier to teach your children to study hard and just be good like you are, but how good are you really?"

"Speaking of good," Don said. "A good starting point would be to study what everyone's arguing about, and think, rather than start off thinking you know everything."

"If only the freeking terrorists would read the *Sermon on the Mount*," Fonu said. "They might understand that even the thought of murdering people was bad."

"Just think if a terrorist really understood the importance of their thoughts," Don said, closing his eyes to think for a moment. "Imagine a terrorist coming to the realization that their bad thoughts were really bad, just like the Buddha and Jesus taught! Just imagine! There they'd be, with all these bad thoughts about Jews, Christians, Atheists and gay people popping into their heads. I don't think they'd be very happy. On the contrary, I think they'd be mad at the way they were brainwashed."

"Hopefully, they'd get mad enough to kill all the other terrorists in their group, including their leaders, problem solved," Fonu said.

"Fonu!" Don exclaimed. "Getting them to understand the *Sermon on the Mount*, so they'll go on a killing spree, isn't the point!" Don said, laughing a little.

"If Muslims get to talk at church in the park, I'd have something to say too," Fonu Ali said. "I'd tell everyone about my father getting trampled to death during the Hajj of 2015. That might wake someone up and get them to start studying what everyone's arguing about and think."

"Then, maybe one day, we'll all get together at the park and give thanks and help others," Abe said. "That's about the only thing I think everyone can agree on. Muslims, Christians, Atheists and Jews, Buddhists, Zoroastrians, Mormons and Hindus, all believe helping others is good."

Donna stood up like an activist leader and said, "Especially helping our children by protecting them from predators and organizations who try to brainwash us to think bad thoughts about our neighbors."

"Donna makes an excellent point regarding organizations and the importance of discerning the spirit of the organization," Larry said. "Therefore, we need to look closely at what an organization teaches. If they teach us or our children to think less of another group of people, then it's an evil organization. They may say they're super-duper Biblical or super-duper liberal. If they're teaching children to look down or have bad thoughts toward their gay or Christian neighbor, then they're doing the work of the devil."

"We'll have fundamentalists teaming up with gay activists to protect our children from pedophiles," Don said. "And we'll have moderate Christians, Muslims and Jews working to protect our children from religious and political extremists. And everyone will help those in need at the park."

"If anyone needs to be rescued, they can go to the park!" Larry exclaimed.

"If anyone wants to help others," Abe said. "They can go to the park and join in with others helping others."

Donna looked at Larry and then Don. *If we had a Church in the Park, I could have gone to the park for help. These guys might be on to something. I might be into this Church in the Park idea. Maybe not all churches are like the one I grew up with?* Then she asked, "Will everyone get a chance to speak at *Church in the Park*?"

"Even gay, bisexual, transgender and queer, Mormons, Muslims, Jehovah's Witnesses and Jews?" Gerry asked.

"Yes, everyone will get to speak at some point," Don said. "But first, they need to admit the possibility they might be wrong. If they can't admit this possibility, then they're the ones causing the insanity, so they don't get the microphone.

They've had it for much too long. Now, they'll have to listen. And hopefully, they'll learn something.

"Newcomers should listen and visit with others, and then sign up if they want to speak. Everyone will be encouraged to share their experiences that resulted in how they now believe. People can share stories of death and strife that changed their life, stories of prayers that were answered, stories of joy and supernatural dreams, stories of experiences that helped them break through their brainwashing."

"Can atheists share too?" Donna asked.

"Of course, as long as they can admit the possibility they might be wrong," Don said. "Dave's my favorite atheist. And just like Dave, atheists are some of the best people, with great stories about why they're atheist."

"What about Satanists?" Gerry asked.

"I have an opinion," Don said, turning to Larry. "But I'm curious what Larry thinks?"

"Yes, of course, Satanists too," Larry said. "Jesus came to save sinners, and Satanists sure love to sin. So of course, Satanists should be invited to share."

"I agree," Don said. "As long as they can admit the possibility they might be wrong. Most likely, they're just naturally disobedient and rebellious like the rest of us. Satanists like to wear red and black and pentagrams around their neck for shock value, but it's hard to believe they actually worship and give thanks to Satan. Satan can perform magic tricks, but he can't do miracles, so his following will be just as false as his power and lies. One of the main reasons for *Church in the Park*, is to get people to study what everyone's arguing about. People who've accepted some stupid ass theory or bold-faced lie."

"I'm sure the Satanist will have an interesting theory explaining why their sin isn't really sin anyway," Larry said. "If you can convince yourself you're not a sinner, you can convince yourself you don't need forgiveness, Jesus, or the Holy Spirit either."

"I look forward to hearing the Satanist's theory," Don said.

"I agree," Larry said. "Everyone should get a chance to speak at some point. People on different paths have been tested in different ways. Even atheists like Dave have a reason why they believe how they believe. Who am I to insist that Dave or Don is a depraved sinner, just because I am."

"Anything's possible with God," Fonu said. "But I'm a sinner like you Larry."

"I love that," Don said. "If people just asked themselves that question and really understood why they believed how they believed, we'd have world peace. If the terrorists really understood why they believed how they believed, they wouldn't go on a killing spree and then kill themselves. If the terrorist's eyes were opened, and they realized, they believed how they believed because of some demented human. If they realized they were brainwashed to believe a lie, and they weren't on the path to paradise, they might wake up to the peaceful path of the meek and loving and get off the hateful path of the mean and bloody."

"They'll be like spiritually blind pirates who now see," Larry said. "Terrorists with murderous thoughts who finally understand the *Sermon on the Mount* will have no problem accepting that they're sinners. The problem for them will be their pride and the pride of their family. It's hard to go against your family."

"A born-again Muslim going against their family should read the Bhagavad Gita," Fonu said. "Arjun was in the spiritual battle we all go through. He was stuck in the deepest depression, because he had close relatives and friends on both sides. At the end of the story, Arjun conquered, because he believed anything was possible with God."

"We'll recommend reading the Bhagavad Gita, the Bible and the Quran to everyone at *Church in the Park*, and we'll study Buddhism too. We'll study them all!" Don exclaimed, with excitement on his face. "I can see it now. We'll have reformed terrorists, with a Bhagavad Gita in one hand and a Bible in the other, with new, peaceful, loving purposes, in parks around the world."

"Only an all loving God with a sense of humor could come up with this," Larry said.

CHAPTER 29

Trina Covina's Secret Got Out

Donna was thinking about Don. She'd never felt this comfortable around a man before. "Do you have a girlfriend Don?" She asked in a soft caring way.

"No girlfriend at this point in time," Don said. "Not since Trina Covina. Remember, the girl from the bully patrol story? I was in love, and I haven't been in love since. And, if it's not love, I'm out."

"Oh yes, I remember," Donna said. "The girl you wanted to impress by fending off the bullies. I thought Fonu said she was a lesbian?"

"As it turned out she was," Don said. "Talk about a test. Trina was a lesbian, and I got her pregnant."

"You got a lesbian pregnant?" Donna asked.

"Yes, we were both only seventeen. The whole thing really messed with my head," Don said, looking deeply in her eyes, thinking about how beautiful she was, even with that big ring in her nose. He loved her sweet face and tight little body. She definitely got Don's motor running.

"Boy or girl?"

"Neither. I don't know," Don replied, pausing to gather himself. "She secretly had an abortion, but my friend's mother worked at the clinic, so her secret got out. Don dropped his head and the whole room went silent. Then he snapped out of it and said, "Then the next week, Dave had his accident, so it was a double test for me back then. I wanted to grow old and wrinkled with Trina. I told her everything, but she never talked about her true feelings with me. It was a bad break-up to say the least.

"Trina was a terrified, closeted, pregnant, seven-teen-year-old lesbian experiencing a calamity, because she had a religious fanatic for a father," Don said. "It's hard to believe she chose death, but I think she could have pleaded insanity.

"Trina's father liked his church exactly the way it was," Don said. "I tried to discuss problems in the church like gay acceptance, but his flippant answer was, 'What problems?' He thought everything was just fine, because it was for him. He wrote me off. He said I was a hell-bound, homo-lover, one of the lost.

"Poor Trina, if only she could've communicated with her father..." Don said, shaking his head slowly. "But she couldn't imagine talking with him about being pregnant at seventeen. She learned time and time again, she just couldn't talk with him about difficult things. It just couldn't be done, because he always had to be one hundred percent right about everything.

"When she was twelve, she asked him if gay people would be in heaven too. His answer was the single word no. In high school, she asked him about gay marriage. He just paraphrased Leviticus 18:22 and said, 'Butt pirates are an abomination to God.' See, says it right here, as he pointed to the Bible. Her father always had the answer to these difficult questions, and he never wasted a minute thinking about how it might affect someone else.

"Trina Covina learned a lot from her father's home brain-washing regiment. Mainly, she learned non-communication. Therefore, when she got pregnant, she went into survival mode. She handled it all by herself. She got an abortion."

Don paused, feeling his strong emotions. "Trina solved her own problem without communication, just like she'd learned growing up. Her father sure knew his Bible, but he didn't have a clue about the importance of communication, especially the part that requires listening. He didn't know that communication held the answer to all problems, even the problem of a girl getting pregnant at seventeen.

"Trina was reared by Bible bumpers, but she never really learned the power of love and forgiveness. She never really understood how important it was to talk about the hard stuff, because that's how a problem gets solved instead of hidden like a dirty secret, left to fester for the rest of one's life.

"Anyway, I haven't had a girlfriend since," Don said, looking at Donna. "I've had dates, but I'm waiting for love before getting hot and heavy again. The gift is, I've had time for other things."

They both looked at Dave, and then Donna looked at Don with a tear rolling down her cheek. She could feel he was hurt deeply ten years ago, but now he was healed and shining again, and she loved him. Don looked a little uncomfortable and said, "Next subject please."

CHAPTER 30

Dons Little Red Book

During all this serious talk, Dave was reading a little red book and giggling about what he was reading.

"Which part are you reading Dave?" Fonu Ali asked.

"The space transport vessel just arrived on Mars," Dave said slowly, as he handed the little red book to Fonu.

"That's my favorite part," Fonu said with a smile.

"Oh no," Don said. "Please, no."

Fonu started reading out loud, "The gigantic spaceship just landed on Mars. It was a huge vessel with another large load of gay men to add to the growing colony of gay men on Mars. It was all a part of the Homosexual Homesteading Act of 2067, wherein gay men on Earth were promised the space party of a lifetime on their one-year cruise to the planet Mars. The deal was, after their yearlong space party, all the gay men agreed to work hard on the new Mars settlement for three years. Afterwards, they would receive a large lump sum payment and another year long party voyage back to Earth, if they pleased. Or, they could remain living in the new gay Mars settlement. Two year-long parties sounded too good to be true. It was an irresistible temptation. How could any gay man refuse?

"After their yearlong party, all the gay men were exhausted. They de-boarded the gigantic spaceship and re-boarded a train that would take them to their final destination. As they were choosing their seats and stowing their luggage, one of the gay men said, 'I guess the party's over fellas.'" Fonu said this, lisping and flailing his wrists.

"'I'm exhausted,' said another. 'I went through my entire one thousand condom allotment.'

"'Me too,' said another. 'I guess they're gonna put us to work now.'

"Just then an announcement came over the loud-speaker, 'This is a homosexual train. All aboard the train to Homosexual City. I understand things are pretty, pretty in Homosexual city.'

"All the gay men on board looked at each other with concern on their faces. 'Did I just hear what I think I heard?' One of the gay men asked.

"'Yes, Yes,' said another. 'They said this was a homosexual train and we were all going to Homosexual City. How could they be that callous? They know we prefer the term gay, calling it Homosexual City is offensive.' All the gay men agreed.

"The Evil Homophobic Genius's plan was alive. He had cameras everywhere on the train, and he was observing everything from the control room on his spaceship. He was rubbing his hands together like it was very cold, and he needed to warm his fingers, but the climate control was working perfectly. He was just an evil genius doing what evil genius's do, rubbing and rubbing his hands together, observing the distressed gay men on the train. 'My plan is working perfectly,' the evil genius said, and then he started singing,

> *'Oh, I'm a homophobe and I'm okay*
> *With another large load of gays on the train*
> *On their way to homosexual city*
> *Little do they know it's not so pretty'*

"The evil genius had a crew of slim, good looking, well-endowed, ex-gay men, who wore tight fitting, multicolored jumpsuits. These men-in-tights ran all the operations on Mars and on the spaceships. And they all adored their evil leader, because he'd cured them of their homosexuality. All it took was good brainwashing, castration and aversive therapy, not necessarily in that order.

"The cure started with brainwashing the gay men to believe their same sex attraction was really, really bad. The next step was much more difficult, because the gay men had to believe their loving thoughts weren't really loving thoughts at all, but something really, really bad too. This step proved difficult to do. So, the evil genius used several types of aversive therapy to accomplish this task.

"His favorite form of aversive therapy was attaching electrodes and pressure sensors to the gay men's junk. Then he'd project holograms of good looking, lean men in seductive poses, all around the room arousing the gay men, triggering the pressure sensors, to signal the micro-controller, to apply a voltage to the electrodes attached to their junk. This therapy helped, but it didn't completely change how the gay men felt about the ones they loved.

"The evil genius' final solution was brainwashing the gay men to believe castration was the only answer, the only cure for their same sex loving thoughts. Loving thoughts that really weren't loving at all, but something much, much more evil. The gay men were brainwashed to request castration. That's how effective the evil genius's brainwashing was. They even signed a form requesting to be castrated, absolving their evil leader of any and all liability for this action. It was a perfectly evil plan.

"So now, every year, about a month before Christmas, the evil genius castrates several more thoroughly brainwashed ex-gay men to join his army of abiding unics. He cures and dries their testicles for stringing and hanging on his own private Christmas tree, in his own private quarters on his gigantic spaceship.

"As part of the deal, all the freshly ex-gay men received any size testicle prosthetics they wanted. Of course, they all chose the large size. And they loved the way they looked in their skin-tight jumpsuits. The now well-endowed men-in-tights did the evil genius's bidding on Mars and on his spaceships. They followed his orders explicitly, without a thought or a question. They loved their evil leader so much. They sang songs to show their massive adoration of him.

"After observing the distressed homosexuals on the train to Homosexual City, the evil genius was so happy he couldn't contain himself. The men-in-tights saw his happiness and the look of satisfaction on his face, and this made them happy too. So, they all started singing, like in some kind of weird opera, as they gazed upon the evil leader.

YOU'RE SO BIG

You're so big… so very, very big…
You're so big... and we adore you
We love your bigness...oh...you're so huge
We love your thickness...we love looking at you
You're absolutely immense…..... you're our dude
And we adore you…

"The minions sang songs of adoration for their evil leader, while occasionally glancing at themselves, and their bulging packages, in the walls of the spaceship, polished like a mirror."

"That book's an absolute horror," Gerry said. "Where did you get it Dave?"

"It's Don's *Little Red Book*," Dave replied slowly.

"Where did you get it Don?" Gerry asked.

"I wrote it."

"What?" Donna exclaimed, with her mouth remaining open. "I can't believe it! You wrote that? You wrote that homophobic trash? You actually spent your precious time writing that?"

"I thought we were changing subjects," Don said. "Oh well, I guess now I need to explain my *Little Red Book* too. Yes, I know. It's hard to believe and sad but true. I went through a very homophobic phase after Trina Covina left me. Especially, after I discovered her abortion and saw her kissing that woman. It pushed me off a cliff. You must understand, I was really in love. And at that time, the girl I loved, and our baby were gone. Feel me. I felt all alone. I had just been jilted by a lesbo.

"I felt like a fool, because I thought we communicated so well. Her solo decision killed me in here," Don said pointing to his heart. "She destroyed our creation without even talking with me about it. I totally didn't get it. I loved her so much. Why couldn't she at least talk with me about it? That's what made me even more sad, knowing she had to deal with it all alone. Or, if she wasn't alone, who was she talking to? The abortionists?

"I was badly hurt, and I knew I was in a spiritual battle. So, I started going to a local church. It was one of those churches, like Larry experienced, with a lot of homophobes with hot wives, and lots of little kids. So, I turned into a homophobe for a while, although I insisted I wasn't. You know it's true. You become who you hang with. Well, today I'm hanging with you," Don said, looking at Donna hoping she could understand.

"You were a raging homophobe?" Donna asked. "I can't believe it."

"Well, maybe not raging," Don replied. "But I was a very emotional homophobe for a while, that's for sure. And I write when I'm emotional. I can't help it. Writing's my therapy, and my little red book is what came out. Believe it! You might say I committed a crime of passion in my mind at the time, but since then, I've had my homophobic awakening. Just think of me as one of the guys being thoroughly gratified by an elaborate effing machine. And I wasn't the flaming mo."

"You Don, a raging Bible Bumper?" Gerry asked. "I can't believe it. Really Don, you? You're way too cool."

"Yes! I was traumatized by a lesbian, and I wrote that book. And I laughed like a friggin' evil genius while I wrote it," Don said. "It was my therapy. Why can't anyone believe me? I was a homophobe for about a year and a half. At the time, I went a little crazy."

"You're too brilliant to be a homophobe," Gerry said.

"I'm not a homophobe anymore!" Don said emphatically. "I told you. I had my awakening."

"I'm thsorry, I'm just in a thstate of shock," Gerry lisped, crossing his legs like a woman. "You're way too good looking."

"Can you believe a person who survived a terrorist attack could become afraid of terrorists or people that remind them of terrorists?" Don asked.

"Yes, at least for a while," Donna said.

"Okay, so loosen the noose," Don said. "People change when they learn things. And people change again when they realize part of what they learned was wrong. The main thing I learned was, something only needs to be one percent wrong to be wrong.

"So, believe it!" Don exclaimed. "I became a homophobe for a while. I went to a one Bible fits all, non-questioning Church, and I hung out with homophobes with hot wives. The good part was, I learned a lot about the Bible, and everything was about ninety-nine percent true. The problem was, they were demonizing Trina, and I knew that was wrong."

"That's similar to my experience Don."

"I know Larry. It's kind of spooky. Anyway, I studied the Bible a lot with these guys, and on my own, and with Fonu of course, and it all led to my homophobic awakening. So, the story has a happy ending. You see, at one point, I realized I was having new bad thoughts popping into my head. I realized my thoughts were changing for the worse.

"I learned from Buddhism to be mindful of my thoughts, and I've always been especially mindful of the bad thoughts that tend to pop into my head now and then. Well, at the time, I started having new bad thoughts popping into my head whenever I encountered obviously gay men.

"You see, I've always been aware of these bad thoughts, and I still have them," Don said, looking at Donna and then putting his head down for a second. "Mostly, it's when I see mean looking people. I immediately judge them in my thoughts, and I know it's wrong. Maybe they're not even mean. Maybe they just look mean or their face is just frozen or something.

"Like one time at the train station, I saw this big, mean looking, tuff guy scratching his crotch like crazy. He was pacing back and forth, stopping and scratching, and then pacing some more, and then stopping again to scratch his junk. He was a big, lean, six-foot stud with huge muscles, but he looked mean, like a man who used women and spit them out. I felt happy inside, like there was justice in the world that day, because he had crabs or an STD or something. It made me happy to see him suffer. I enjoyed watching him scratch. I'm so bad up here sometimes," Don said, putting his index finger to his head. "Maybe he was really a nice guy."

"Or, this time on the bus, a mean looking banger was talking loud about getting out of prison and bragging to his homey about partying and having sex with some local girl named Jez. His homey on the bus knew Jez. His homey said, 'Oh man, you did it with Jez? I hope you wrapped it up Holmes. She got diseases.' The mean looking banger went silent. He looked like he might vomit at any moment, because he didn't use a condom. 'You better get checked out,' his homey said. I smiled in my thoughts and giggled inside. I knew my thoughts were bad.

"You see, I've been trying to control these bad thoughts my entire life," Don said, shaking his head. "They usually pop up when I see a mean looking tough guy with a miserable expression on his face. Automatically I think, serves you right mean dumbass, try being friendly for a change, smiling is not a sign of weakness.

"I've always been aware of these bad thoughts. I ask God to take them away, but I still have them. And since being plugged into the church of the homophobes with hot wives, I realized I was having new bad thoughts popping into my head whenever I encountered obviously gay men. I knew bad thoughts were bad, therefore I knew something was wrong.

"At first, I believed all these homophobic guys," Don said. "It was a church group, not an evil organization, right? And they really knew their Bible. And they had good jobs and hot wives, but when it came to explaining the whole gay acceptance thing, all they had were the same canned answers they learned from their pastor. 'We don't discriminate,' they said. 'We look at homosexuals no differently than hopeless alcoholics or heroin addicts.'"

"I don't know about anyone else," Larry interjected. "I only know about me. And when I was using drugs, I preferred to keep it out of sight and hidden in the darkness. So, if a gay couple wants to get married and be monogamous and announce it to the world and shine the light on it, that doesn't fit the description of sin to me. The Bible says sin is something we want to keep in the shadows, away from the light."

"What turned the light on for me," Don said, "was the, 'Is it possible' question I asked the pastor. I asked him, 'Is it possible a single gay couple could exist that loved each other how God intended people to love each other in marriage?' "

"That question sounds like Abraham's questions to God," Larry interjected. "You know, regarding Sodom and Gomorrah in Genesis 18:23. Abraham was questioning God about possibly destroying some righteous along with the wicked in Sodom and Gomorrah."

"It's a parallel question," Don said. "That's my point. God and Abraham were batting the question back and forth for quite a while, but this pastor didn't need a minute to think. 'No,' the pastor replied, flashing back to his single indiscretion in the Navy. He couldn't imagine such a thing could possibly be loving. He couldn't imagine, imagining the possibility. To him, all gay people were either mentally ill, deceived by Satan, or evil geniuses with bleached anuses, possessed by demons, who want to molest our children and turn the whole world gay. The pastor wouldn't even consider my, 'Is it possible' question. He said he was very concerned. He said the question sounded like it came from a demon.

"You know," Don said. "Sometimes the smartest people do the stupidest things, like believing homophobic things without studying human sexuality. So, I started studying what everyone was arguing about. I started studying the whole gay and transgender thing. And I slowly came to the conclusion, I had been brainwashed."

CHAPTER 31

Hardwired Gay from the Get-go

"Don?" Gerry asked.

"Yes Gerry."

"Was this when you had your homophobic awakening?" And then he put a finger to his lips.

"Yes, it was just about this time, Fonu and I both had our homophobic awakenings," Don replied. "The tipping point came after we talked with this gay guy we met on the bus. His name was Fernando, and he was obviously gay because of his fancy hairdo and the way he was dressed. We introduced ourselves and explained how we were studying everything gay and would like to talk with him. He was thrilled, and he was so nice, we invited him over for a beer."

"What? You mean I'm not your first?" Gerry asked.

"Sorry Gerry," Don replied, shaking his head. "No, but Fernando was very happy we were studying gay stuff, and he was very willing to talk with us. He told us all about himself. He told us how he'd always thrown like a girl, and he was bad at hitting too, so he always got picked last. And when he finally got picked, the mean kids would say, 'Oh no, not Fagenbaum.' His last name was Tannenbaum, but the bullies called him Fagenbaum. This made him sad, and we felt sad too listening to his story that day.

"He was eighteen when he came out of his transparent closet. He told everyone he was gay, and he was in love with a young man his same age. He was so proud. He wanted to share it with the world. He was especially proud, the guy he loved could pitch like a real man, not throw like a girl, like him."

"Did they both catch too?" Gerry asked, with a devious smile, as Fonu looked at him with a disgusting look on his face.

"Thank you, Gerry. That comment adds a whole new dimension to our homophobic awakenings. Anyway, after our talk with Fernando and a lot of studying, we concluded the gay acceptance problem could be boiled down to love centered vs. sex centered thinking. And, don't forget, our words reveal our thoughts," Don said, looking at Gerry. "You see, the gay activist extreme is too sex centered rather than love centered, which causes the church to be sex centered too, concerning marriage, when they should be love centered."

"I know," Larry said. "The gay extreme seems more about promoting the gay lifestyle, promiscuity, and the all sex is good mentality. Don calls it sex centered. I'd just call it worldly, or the pleasure centered mentality, which has nothing to do with the vows of marriage.

"What Don calls love centered thinking, sounds to me like the good old-fashioned waiting, until you fall in love kind of thinking. Waiting, until you find that special someone you want to share your life with. Waiting, and then making a commitment in front of friends, before the lovemaking.

"This may sound prudish," Larry said, turning to Donna. "But how do you know if a man, who says he's in love with you, really is in love with you?"

Donna felt put on the spot. She knew Larry couldn't read her mind, but she was thinking about Don at that exact time. She was having strong feelings for him, like maybe she was falling in love. She was so full of emotions, she couldn't think. So, she just blurted out, "I don't know Larry. How can I tell if a man who says he's in love with me, really is?"

"This would apply to gay men too, wouldn't it Larry?" Gerry asked.

"Yes, this would apply to gay men too Gerry," Larry said. "How can you tell if a gay man, who says he's in love with you, really is, in love with you?"

"I don't know. I can't read his mind," Gerry replied.

"I don't know either," Donna said.

"Don't have sex with him," Larry said. "In time you'll know, because all the men who only wanted sex will have left. After a year or two, if he's still there, I'd say he really loves you."

There was silence in the room. Larry had just spoken a piece of wisdom, and everybody knew it. Donna and Gerry especially knew it, because they'd both been hurt by guys who lied about being in love. Guys who only wanted sex.

"What, no sex?" Gerry asked.

"For a couple of years?" Donna chimed in. "Isn't that kind of extreme?"

"If you want to be certain the man who says he's in love with you, really is," Larry said. "No sex before marriage has its benefits. That's why there's so much fuss in the Bible about circumcision. It's to teach us not to be so sex centered. Like Don said, being love centered is where it's at."

"I think the sex would be better too," Donna said. "Just knowing he really loved me and wanted to share his life with me." The entire room went silent again for what seemed like a long ten seconds.

"Back to the gay boy you invited over for a beer," Gerry said, breaking the silence.

"Where were we," Don said, still thinking about Donna. "Oh yea, well, Fernando taught us a lot, but the main thing I got was how he felt growing up. He grew up feeling unloved and ashamed of who he was. And no child should grow up feeling like that!" Don exclaimed. "Fernando felt ashamed he was gay, ashamed of living a lie and ashamed of covering up how he really felt inside. So, when he finally came out, he made a vow to be mentally healthy and never deny his gayness again. We learned a lot from Fernando. He was definitely hardwired gay from the get-go."

"And look how you guys have grown," Gerry said. "Now you've accepted me into your life too. It's like a fairy tale ending."

"You're thinking rear ending? I know," Fonu said, with a grimace on his face.

"Fonu! Quit making faces!" Don exclaimed, like he was scolding a bad dog. "Anyway, we learned a lot from Fernando and all our studies. We learned some gay people fall in love and get married and have children and love God and have loving thoughts while they're having sex, just like some heterosexual people do, except they do it without vaginas or penises as the case may be.

"We also learned some gay people get married and are bad and selfish and raise screwed up kids, just like some heterosexual people do. So, we concluded, acceptance shouldn't be based on sexual orientation, acceptance should be based on if people were love-centered or not."

"Too bad we can't read minds," Larry said.

"We learned about transgender people too," Fonu said. "They suffer from gender dysphoria, so they want to use a different bathroom than one would expect by looking at their plumbing."

"Fonu!" Don exclaimed. "It's so much more complicated than that. But the bathroom laws of the past are a perfect example of people who professed to be experts, but who knew very little about human sexuality. Gender dysphoria is a very distressing feeling transgender people experience. For example, a transgender man who feels like a man, and looks like a man, and probably has a beard like a man, wants to use the men's room even though he has a vagina. He and other people will feel distress, if he's forced to use the lady's room, because he looks like a man. Transgender people have to deal with much more than just using the restroom. They have to deal with living on the same planet with know-it-alls-who-don't-know-it-all."

"We learned about inter-sex people too," Fonu said. "Like people who were born with a vagina and have testicles inside.

Or, people who were born with a super small penis and a vagina. Or, people who were born with a penis with an opening in the shaft instead of the tip, what a trip. I never realized all the screwed-up ways God makes people."

"I know, and they say I wasn't born gay," Gerry said. "Who do they think they're fooling?"

"It wasn't long after studying everything gay, that we came up with our *Insertion Theory*," Don said. "It explains why there'll be gays in heaven. First, we postulated that a truly loving, gay, monogamous married couple could exist. Then we considered how the Old Testament verses in Leviticus, condemning anything even slightly gay, could also be true. We refused to start off by throwing out the books a whole lot of people believed to be supernatural."

"So, rather than throw out the Bible entirely," Fonu said, excitedly. "And because it's possible that well-meaning men inserted a verse or two or three. People should feel free to look at the Bible as a buffet. People should feel free to throw out or de-insert any insanity provoking books or verses."

"While being ever mindful of our thoughts," Don said, pointing up.

"A buffet Fonu?" Gerry asked, in a slow deep voice.

"This goes perfectly with my theory," Larry said. "That the Bible was written by heterosexuals, with heterosexuals in mind, because at the time, the world was ninety-nine percent heterosexual. As time progressed, and the earth got more and more over-populated, more and more gay people were born as a form of population control. And today, about seven percent of people are born hardwired gay.

"As a heterosexual man thinking selfishly, I have no issues with the Bible as written," Larry continued. "It's easy to understand from the hardwired heterosexual male point of view. I agree that, for me, having sex with a man would be against my nature and it would be bad. But I also believe in what Jesus taught, so I'm trying not to think selfishly.

"I also understand, God makes people very different than I am, and I realize that some words in the Bible, literally interpreted, don't sit too well for a gay person or a woman who wants to be a preacher, or this or that. I totally get people who are repulsed by organized religion. Therefore, I too am repulsed by organized religion. Maybe repulsed is too harsh a word. I just bought my own personal rescue vehicle, rather than giving my money to the church."

"As recent as the last century, the church was demonizing inter-racial marriages too," Don said, "and women who wanted to wear pants, and people who only wanted to dance."

"In the roaring twenties," Larry said. "The Church was producing active prohibitionists. They were mostly women who saw the demon in their alcoholic husbands. Women who experienced evil up close and personal, and it helped them believe in God. So, they studied their Bible like their life depended on it, and soon, they realized they had God's special knowledge in their hands. Too bad that special knowledge went to their heads before they could understand 1Corinthians 8:2 warning us not to become know-it-alls.

"The problem was, when they asked God for help, they already knew the answer. They knew alcohol was bad for everyone, period! No exceptions. So, they searched the scriptures for verses that supported their theory. They were on a mission from God now, to eliminate bars, school dances and all alcohol everywhere.

"From their experiences, these women knew alcohol was bad for their husbands. Therefore, they wanted it outlawed for everyone's benefit. But they were wrong, and history has proven, prohibition won't work in America. And Islamic Sharia Law, prohibiting alcohol and a lot of other things, won't work in America either, because God wants us to have free will. It's another main theme from the Bible a lot of people just don't get," Larry said.

"It seems we've come full circle on this," Don said. "Now, I look at my homophobic past as a little story within the big story of my life. It's not too pretty, but it's part of who I am. It's part of my life of learning. Now, I look at my *Little Red Book* as one insane little book in the big book of my life, similar to how Leviticus is one little book in the Bible."

"I know," Larry said. "If one reads a gay clobber verse, like Leviticus 18:22, standing alone and out of context, it doesn't appear to belong in God's Story of Love. When taken out of its heterosexual context, some parts of the Bible can appear like they were written by an evil homophobic genius."

"Or a control freak," Gerry said.

"Yes," Don said, looking at Donna. "So please, don't let my *Little Red Book* define me today, without knowing my whole story, without knowing me and where my heart is today, or you'll get me wrong and out of context."

"It's like someone only reading the Old Testament, and then dismissing the entire Bible as conceived by evil Jewish geniuses trying to control the masses," Larry said. "A lot of very smart people don't understand - the Jewish leaders lost control of the masses after the death of Jesus, exactly as the supernatural scriptures, they didn't understand, predicted.

"And when Jesus said, 'It is finished,' as He died on the cross and then He rose three days later," Larry said. "It was the ending of God's supernatural story. And Jesus' death scattered many Jewish people just like the Bible predicted. Then, after Hitler slaughtered millions of Jews during the second world war, the state of Israel was officially formed in 1948, and more and more Jews returned to join the Jews who never left, also as predicted in the Bible."

"Humans easily capitulate to what the world wants them to believe," Fonu said. "Most are too lazy to try to understand the whole story, especially the end of the story, for themselves."

"I absolutely love that Larry," Gerry said. "If Leviticus was written by an evil genius, the Bible makes perfect sense now. And what about Paul? Do you think Paul was an evil homophobic genius too?"

"Larry didn't say anyone was an evil genius Gerry," Don said. "He said if it was taken out of its heterosexual context it could appear...You're a psychiatrist Gerry. I know you're intelligent enough to understand this."

CHAPTER 32

GINTCOI

"I may be a doctor Don, but I'm gay," Gerry said. "And I could never understand those terrible things Paul wrote about me in the Bible. Jesus never said those kind of mean things, but Paul made me feel bad about the loving feelings I had. It nearly drove me mad. Thank God my survival instincts kicked in. Too bad, I had to leave my faith to survive."

"I'm sorry," Abe said. "That's so sad."

"How could I believe in something that was driving me mad?" Gerry said. "At the time, I needed to cure myself, so I turned to psychology. Jung and Freud became my best friends. I needed to cure the insanity I felt as a young gay man growing up in a fundamentalist Christian family. And, I wanted to understand why I was attracted to large, sweaty, harry, bearded men," Gerry said, looking at Abe and smiling.

"We all want to understand crazy things that changed our lives," Don said. "Abe wants to understand why he got thighed as a child. Fonu wants to understand why his father was killed so tragically and why he survived. Dave wants to understand why a tree killed his entire family, and why another tree gave him a partial lobotomy. I really want to understand why Dave still loves trees after all he's been through. I really want to understand that."

"It's okay," Dave said, smiling contently.

"I know, especially really, really bad things," Larry said, "that seem inconsistent with an all-powerful, infinitely loving God in control of everything. At these times, just remember—GINTCOI—God Is Not The Creator Of Insanity."

"I was sure feeling the insanity," Don said. "So, after my homophobic awakening, I went back to church and shared everything I'd learned during our research. I shared how I was especially concerned about the high transgender and gay suicide rate, and how it was positively correlated to the degree of shame, non-acceptance and non-love a person experienced at home, school and church.

"The pastor had the answer as usual. He said the homosexual suicide statistics were inflated by the liberal media, and the especially high suicide rate for transvestite people was a total fabrication. He emphasized the word transvestite, which is an insult to a transgender person. What? Did he think I was an idiot?" Don said, with his eyes open wide. "If I was transgender with a parent like you, I'd probably be thinking some weird stuff too."

"I know," Fonu said, "If my father was alive, and I was a big, fat, hairy chick with a you know what, he'd have honor killed me before I had the chance to kill myself. The suicide statistics make perfect sense to me. How could a church lie like that?"

"Because they're only thinking about how the Bible relates to them," Don said. "A lot of hard-core church cats have tunnel vision. They can't feel someone who's very different, so they pass on some lie they heard from someone just like them. They stay in their comfort zone, instead of thinking a little differently. And by teaching this lie, they're teaching hatred, and their missionaries are exporting hatred around the world and saying it's God's truth. That's why I can't hang with super religious church cats, and I'd rather have *Church in the Park*."

"Many super religious people have the Bible nearly memorized, but somehow they miss the main themes," Larry said. "They miss the concept of love at its deepest and the radical concept of loving one's enemy, which simply means loving people different than you. They miss the overall teaching that the law can't be written in stone. That's why Jesus broke so many Jewish laws, like eating with non-Jews and sinners, and healing on the Sabbath, but many super religious people don't see this. They don't seem to get it!"

"Many Church leaders are blind," Don said. "Similar to the Jewish Pharisees who believed they were God's chosen ones."

"Jesus taught us how wrong these Pharisees were and how radical God's love was," Larry said. "The Jewish Pharisees wanted to, and finally did, kill Jesus. Today, it's like the fundamentalist leaders are trying to kill the church.

They're making God's love appear repulsive to many sensitive, caring people, trying their best to be good."

"Today, people have experienced their own truths," Don said. "Like having loving gay friends who got married and were monogamous. People have also experienced loud hyper-masculine fundamentalist types, professing to be experts on everything gay."

"People reject the rigid as stone thinking because it's wrong," Donna said.

"So, they throw out baby Jesus with the homophobic bathwater," Dave said slowly.

"Yes Dave," Don said. Then Fonu started playing a tune.

I'D RATHER BE WRONG
If the fundamentalists are right
I would rather be wrong
I could not live in peace
while causing in–san–i–ty
I would rather go to hell with my friends
than take the side of a bully

"But the good news is," Larry said, looking at Abe. "Once the fundamentalists realize they've been brainwashed, they can get re-brainwashed with love."

"Yes," Don said, looking at Donna. "You know, I think women could help change everything, because a man in love with a pretty girl will become a homophobic Christian or an animal activist, if that's what it takes to get her. Women are so important, because they've got the power. Muslim women, Christian and Hindu women, all women need to exert their power and study what people are arguing about and teach it to their men."

"And don't just read one sacred book," Fonu Ali said. "Read the Bhagavat Gita too, and pray and meditate, and try to communicate with God."

"And find your purpose," Larry said. "Your mission. Your good big goal like Don's always talking about. And I'll tell you one thing for certain," Larry said, looking at Donna seriously. "Your big goal isn't just pleasing your husband and believing exactly how he and all your friends believe. It's going to be scarier than that. This is God we're talking about! And being led by God, nothing is certain except change, and that you'll be blown away.

"Admitting we need to change is just the beginning to understanding the mysteries of peace and healing in the Bible. It doesn't matter if you're straight, gay, bisexual or transgender. You can fully understand this special knowledge. It begins with being able to see your badness in the mirror."

"You certainly can bring on the message Larry," Abe said. "Everybody wants special knowledge, peace and healing."

"Thanks Abe," Larry said. "I get carried away sometimes."

"Larry can bring the message at *Church in the Park*," Don said, with a smile, "Our new good big goal."

"I really like how you included the women," Donna said, looking at Don and then Larry. "And thinking for yourself. And if it sounds insane toss it out."

"And having a good big goal is good for you," Don said.

"But how do you know how big of a goal to set for yourself," Donna asked. "A big goal that's too big or too difficult, could get frustrating. That's how I feel when I think about starting a *Church in the Park*."

CHAPTER 33

How Big is Big?

"Not doing something can't be your good big goal in life," Don said. "Not smoking or not drinking or not eating too much is good for your health, but it can't be your good big goal. It's just not big enough. You need to really do something for it to be a good big goal."

Donna was getting more and more infatuated with Don as he explained all these deep matters so clearly. "It's like you're working on all the problems in the world," Donna said. "It's so cool. How'd you come up with your theory?"

"Look," Fonu jumped in. "We came up with our theory while we were helping Dave after his partial lobotomy. We all moved in together with the good big goal of helping Dave get better.

"Fixing up this place and helping Dave was a lot of work, especially those first few years. Starting the cult was a lot of work too. Then, one day we noticed Dave was getting a lot better, and after a couple more years, Don and I realized we were the happiest we ever were.

"Don was the one who connected our happiness to helping Dave, which was our first good big goal. So, we thought about what another good big goal could be, like eliminating war and violence. What seemed insane to us was, people everywhere abhorred war and violence. People everywhere wanted peace. So, why was there war and violence? We realized, it wasn't the people. It was the political groups and organizations. It was the governments and the media. It was the military like corporations and organized religions that were the problem. Specifically, it was the secrets they held, secrets they didn't want people like us to know.

"We started with the Catholics," Fonu said, "because everyone knows Catholics kept a lot of secrets. Our new good big goal became eliminating what seemed insane about religion…"

"Rather than eliminating God from the equation," Don interjected. "And we didn't want to eliminate the law. We wanted to apply the spirit of the law like Jesus taught, so as not to cause insanity for anyone. Like, just imagine being a gay person in love and asking the advice of a priest. I guarantee your insanity level would increase dramatically. Hearing the priest suggest lifelong celibacy might wake you up like an ice-cold water full bucket dose of reality. Was the priest crazy? Was he driven crazy by his own attempt at celibacy?

"Then you ask another priest and get the same answer. Soon you discover, one is just like another, and they all don't have a good answer, as they continue to label gay marriages illegitimate, just like they used to label children. They continue to give the same hurtful advice, while encouraging gay people to live a lie. They don't have a good answer, but they can't admit it."

"They're just toeing the line of church doctrine," Larry said. "With the perfect interpretation of God's word in their heads, they consider gay people the enemy, deceived by Satan, while expending no effort to love them, or really listen to them."

"The Christian right invented words like faggot," Gerry said, looking at Fonu. "And the faces that go with it."

"They curse the deaf by the looks on their faces," Larry said. "Leviticus 19:14."

"And with the signs they hold up saying, 'God hates fags,'" Don said.

"Politics began on the playground," Gerry said, "when some big mean boy called some nice boy, who threw like a girl, a fag. The nice boy went home and asked his mother what the word fag meant. He knew it was bad because of the mean look on the bully's face." Gerry looked at Fonu again.

"The little boy's parents wanted to find the best solution, so they studied up on bullies and everything gay. They knew communication was the answer, so they explained to their little boy all the different ways God makes people. Then, they insisted the school's principal explain the same thing to all the other kids. The little boy's parents had the good big goal of teaching everyone how hurtful words could be. They hung rainbow flags outside their church to announce their acceptance, and they worked on teaching everyone about a small minority of sexually different kids - and so started the Christian left."

"It cracks me up and makes me want to cry at the same time," Larry said. "The Christian right is all upset about this. They say it's their right to choose when to start teaching sex-ed to their kids. The Christian left says you already did! This debate wouldn't be happening if you didn't. You started it all by using the word fag, and by using that word, you taught it to your kid."

"The Christian right needs to step forward and admit they don't have a good answer for the whole gay acceptance thing, because they're not gay," Donna said. "Then we can fix everything. Why can't they just admit the possibility they might have been one percent wrong about what they taught their kids?"

"The Christian right was wrong before," Fonu said. "They used to recommend experimental 'Ex-gay' programs for gay kids. Programs that used aversive therapy on gay kids to make them normal again."

"Fonu are you clueless?" Donna asked. "You can't use the word normal in that context. It's offensive."

"Yes, Fonu. What do you think, I'm abnormal?" Gerry asked. "I'm a triple whammy minority, and I deserve respect. You should refer to yourself as a cis-gender heterosexual rather than normal."

"I am normal," Fonu said, looking at Gerry with one of his contorted faces. "I'm not cis-gender whatever the freek that is. I don't walk around thinking my pooper's a pussy. And I want to know how old Donna is. I think she's underage. We could be in big trouble if she really escaped from a psycho ward, like she said. We could be harboring a fugitive!

I know, it's because she's pretty and thin, so she gets special treatment. She might be a criminal or a murderer or something. We don't even know her last name. We really know nothing about her."

"Fonu, Fonu..." Don said, smiling at Donna. Don liked Donna very much. He felt like she heard every word he said. "I have a good feeling about Donna. I don't think she's a criminal. She's our damsel in distress."

"Don't Fonu, Fonu, me Don. If we end up in jail, who's going to take care of Dave?"

"You have a point there Fonu," Don said, turning to Donna. "Maybe you could tell us a little more about yourself and your situation honey?"

"Here's a little more about myself," Donna said, pulling up her sleeves and exposing her scars.

"She's a cutter! I knew it! She probably belongs in an insane asylum!" Fonu exclaimed. Then he pushed his lips out, worried he might have said something bad.

"Yes, you could say I'm insane," Donna yelled back. And then her voice got softer and more deliberate. "That's what predators always say to their victims who speak up. They say we must be crazy for imagining such a terrible thing. So, it's a double whammy for us.

"First, they abuse us. Then, when we stand up bravely and say something, we're told we're crazy and locked up in an insane asylum. Yes, you could say I'm crazy Fonu, but what about you? Are you sure you're not a perp? At least up here?" Donna asked, placing her index finger on her temple.

Fonu was silent. He felt bad sitting there with his lips pushed out.

"Were the police involved," Don asked gently.

"Yes," Donna replied. "I stabbed my father's friend. But he was touching me and wouldn't stop, so I stabbed him. He denied touching me, and my father told the police chief he believed the perp. My father pointed out my scars and said I was a mentally ill, suicidal, drug addict who wouldn't take her meds. The police chief believed my father, so they put me on a psych hold for seventy-two hours."

"I believe you sweetie," Don said. "You are eighteen, aren't you?"

"Yes Don, I'm eighteen," Donna replied. *At least I will be soon.*

"Donna's the victim," Don said confidently. "Larry rescued her, and we fed her and gave her a place to stay. We're not doing anything wrong Fonu, so don't worry, be happy. Let's play one more and go to bed. It's been a long day."

So, they played one more. Abe and Gerry went home, and Larry Cooley went out to sleep in his rig. Fonu bunked in Dave's room, and Donna slept in Fonu Ali's freshly made bed. Don Sanchez turned his light off, closed his eyes and said, "Thank you for another amazing day." Then he laid down his head.

CHAPTER 34

Two Surprises for Don

The next day was Friday. They all planned to visit Julia in the hospital. Abe Seabrooke and Gerry Long came over about 9:30 and the whole gang went over together in the cult's van. Don was driving with his dark Ray Bands on and the radio was cranking the rock classic *Highway to Hell* by ACDC as they pulled into the parking lot.

When they got to her room, little Julia was breathing on her own and her parents were ecstatic to see Larry again. They hugged him and thanked him over and over for saving their precious little girl.

"I had help," Larry said, as he introduced the group. Everyone was happy because Julia was improving. She was out of intensive care, and she was smiling.

"It was a miracle you were there to save our baby," Julia's father said.

"You are real!" Julia's mother exclaimed, hugging Larry again. "I thought maybe you were an angel, but here you are again in the flesh."

After a while visiting, Julia's mother said, "Larry, I need to ask you something. I need to know why you drive that rescue vehicle? I need to know why you were there to rescue our little girl?"

Larry looked over at Don and raised an eyebrow. Don nodded, because he remembered what Larry said out on the water. Larry never talks about God or Jesus, unless someone asks.

"I went through a very sad and difficult time," Larry said. "I was lost on drugs. I felt bad and all alone, and all I wanted was to die. And I almost did, but then I had an awakening. I suddenly understood why Jesus had to die. It was to teach me how much I was loved and forgiven. Then I got it! I understood, and I really believed I had a life worth living. Now I'm better, because I get it. Now, I'm in the joyful place. And that's why I was there to rescue your daughter."

"Thank you so much Larry," Julia's father said, as he broke down crying with electricity humming through his spine. Julia's parents hugged everyone and cried tears of joy.

Donna felt like she experienced a miracle that day. She realized, she was rescued by this same happy, crazy man in his fire truck from outer space. And she felt like she was changing, like she was here on Earth for a reason, like she was precious too, just like Julia, the little presh-presh in that hospital room.

Everyone received a dose of love that morning. Then the group went home, and Dave made Vietnamese noodle soup for lunch. Afterwards, they played and sang a couple, just like any other day.

The Cult of Food and Dance Incorporated took Thursday and Friday off due to the bombings, but Monday morning they were back in the business of running their food and dance cult. Donna helped out too, and she thought the cult was a kick. On her first day she witnessed over a hundred happy people greeting Abe. Everyone was large, but they were so happy she couldn't believe it. Everyone was beaming. They danced and poked each other gently, as they sang the carrots, apples, beets and cabbage song. "I love carrots, I love apples, I love beets and cabbage too, I love the feeling of hunger pang." They danced, and they sang, "Punch me in the stomach, much another carrot, I love the feeling of hunger pang."

Donna felt happy, as she packed carrots, apples, pickled beets and celery sticks for the members to take with them. She sang and danced and helped make carrots, apples, beets and cabbage salad. She thoroughly enjoyed hearing the stories from all the over-weight people in the cult. They all loved Don because he listened to them. They said they felt connected, like they belonged, and for the first time in their lives, they found it easy to lose weight.

This went on for several months, and Donna felt truly happy. She enjoyed working in the cult, and singing the carrots, apples, beets and cabbage song, and she knew she was in love with Don. She loved his smell and how he hugged and seemed to love everyone, and when he hugged her she melted.

Don was unusually comfortable with human touch. This was because of nine months he spent in the hospital when he was young, recovering from his tragic brain injury. There was a certain Catholic nun who visited Don every day. It was like she was there all the time. She sang to him and prayed. She stroked his forehead and caressed his arms. She hugged him a lot, because she believed in the power of love, healing prayer and healing touch. And Don received a healing while he was in there.

When Don left the hospital, his brain had been miraculously changed. He walked out with a very advanced brain, and he just couldn't stop hugging people. He hugged people he'd barely just met. Don Sanchez wasn't much for just a handshake, without at least a half hug. He comfortably put his arms around people, loving them with his calming touch, and Donna loved that about him.

One night, after everyone went to bed, Donna was thinking about how much she loved Don. *It had been four months?* So, she took the big dark ring out of her nose and quietly went into Don's room. Don woke up and saw her standing in the moonlight. She looked so beautiful, like an angel, and then he noticed she didn't have the ring in her nose. Don stood up, just as Donna dropped her robe. They embraced and fell back into Don's bed. He told her he loved her, and they made love and fell asleep in each other's arms.

Very early the next morning, there was a knock at the front door. Dave opened it to find two police officers and Larry standing there. The police were investigating a missing underage girl. They asked for the owner of the house, so Larry and Dave went in to get Don. They approached Don's bedroom door just as Donna was coming out. She was embarrassed to see Larry and Dave there, so she quickly shut Don's door, said good morning, and went to her room.

"Did you see that!" Dave said slowly. "She took it out!"

"Yes, I did," Larry said. They both noticed Donna had taken the ring out of her nose. They knew something was up.

Don rose from his bed feeling great. He felt in love again. Then he flashed back to Trina Covina, his first love, and the first time they did it. He felt the same way with her back then. He put on some jeans and a tee shirt and opened his door to find Dave and Larry standing there. "She was our damsel in distress," Larry said.

Don didn't know how Dave and Larry knew, but they knew. "I love her," Don said. "Isn't that what matters. What's up Larry?"

"The cops are at the door looking for a missing underage girl," Larry said.

"Underage? Oh crap," Don said.

Don went to the front door and greeted the police standing there. Larry and Donna came out too, followed by Dave and Fonu. Don was the owner of the house, so they had to bring him in for questioning.

At that moment, Dr. Gerry Long came running over with his wrists flailing in the air saying, "My word, my word, what's the emergency? Oh my, you brutes have Don in handcuffs! Stop that! He's the best!"

The police confirmed, Donna was the girl they were looking for. She really did escape from a psycho ward. They put her in a straitjacket and took them both down to the police station.

CHAPTER 35

The Highest Rated
Show in the Universe

At the police station, Don Sanchez was taken to an interrogation room. He was left there for twenty minutes or so. Then, two detectives came in. One was young, thin, tall and didn't speak. The other was average height, about fifty, and bordering on obese. "So, Mr. Don Sanchez, what is it you like to do?" The portly detective asked.

"What? What kind of question is that?" Don asked back.

"We're from the human trafficking task force. I'm detective Jensen, and I suggest you answer all my questions."

"Human trafficking? Okay, I'll answer your questions," Don said. "I like to play piano and sing with my friends Fonu and Dave."

"Are you the owner of the property where we found the missing minor?"

"Yes," Don replied.

"Why were you holding an underage girl in your home?"

"You ask that like I was holding her captive!" Don exclaimed, feeling attacked. "I'm not holding her. She's with us by her own free will. The truth is, my friend Larry rescued her, and we were helping her. And she was helping us run the business."

"In detective school, they taught us to listen deeply when a perp says, 'The truth is,'" detective Jensen said, with quoting fingers in the air. "You said, the truth is, you were helping her, and she was helping you run a business? What's the name of your business?"

"No, wait! I'm not a perp!" Don exclaimed. "I didn't say that! I said the truth is WE were helping her, and she was helping US run the business. It wasn't me. It was we! We and us, not me and her. The business was to help Dave get brain surgery. That's the truth."

"Okay, I heard you, Mr. Sanchez. But you didn't answer my question. What's the name of your business?" Detective Jensen asked.

"*The Cult of Food and Dance Incorporated,*" Don said, lowering his head. He knew he was screwed.

"You actually admit you're a cult leader?"

"I'd like to consult a lawyer please," Don said. *These guys are dead serious, and I just admitted to running a cult. They don't care that it was started for a good cause. It's still a cult. And, if Donna is a minor working for us, how could I explain? And, if they find my DNA, they're going to put me away.*

Don knew his loving thoughts weren't going to save him. *Who was going to rescue me? Fonu? Dave? Gerry? Abe? Larry, in his fire truck from outer space? How were the cops ever going to understand?*

"She's seventeen Mr. Don Sanchez, and you're twenty-eight," Detective Jensen said. "That clearly breaks the half your age plus seven rule, so I think you're in big trouble. You're going to be with us overnight, at least, until the rape kit and toxicology reports are in. Stand up, you're coming with me. You better pray we don't find any drugs or semen."

"She said she was eighteen," Don said.

"Oh really? I never heard that one before," Detective Jensen said sarcastically, as he led Don down a long corridor. They came to another room where Don was put inside all alone. It was a cold room with a small window in the door and a single long bench leading to a barrier with a toilet behind it. At first, Don stood there with his hands in his pockets as he talked with his understanding of God. "Dear God of heavens armies, the one and only loving source we all come from, it's me," Don said, with his eyes squeezed shut. "Thank you for putting Donna in my life and thank you for Dave getting better, but what's with the roller coaster ride? Please, wake me up if I'm sleeping. Or, is this another test? If so, now I'm asking for help. Please God, help me out of this mess."

Don thought about Donna and how beautiful she was without that big ring in her nose. It was ecstasy to agony for him. He couldn't believe it. *How could I end up here*? He paced in small circles for twenty or thirty minutes. Then he sat on the hard floor and meditated until his legs went numb.

He sat on the long bench and waited for what seemed like seven or eight more hours.

He laid down on the bench and stared at the ceiling. He felt very tired and was thinking about sleeping, when suddenly a man appeared. He was dressed very businesslike, in a light gray suit, thin black tie and white shirt. He was very slim, stood five foot seven and wore a gray hat trimmed with a black ribbon. He held a black pad in one hand and twirled a golden stylus in the other. Altogether, he looked like a stereotypical, old fashioned news reporter. Don sat up, rubbed his eyes and asked, "Where did you come from man?"

"It's an honor Don," the man replied, extending his hand in greeting. "My name is Blake, and I'm from the *Earth Observer Daily*. It's truly a pleasure to meet you. I just love you, Fonu, Dave, and the whole gang. I simply love all of you."

"How the hell did you get in here?" Don asked. "I wasn't asleep. You just materialized before my eyes."

"Yes, I did Don. You're correct on that," Blake said. "I can't lie to the famous Don Sanchez."

"I don't believe it," Don said. "Do it again."

Blake disappeared and then reappeared on the other side of the room.

"How do you know Fonu and Dave?" Don asked.

"I've been watching you guys ever since the day you bumped into Larry floating in the ocean. That was four months plus one day ago. It was the day your show was rated one thousandth in the universe."

"Yes, I remember that day," Don said. "I met both Larry and Donna that day."

"And you came back with an answer that day too, remember?" Blake asked.

"Yes, Muhammad had a point," Don replied.

"Exactly," Blake said. "Since then, *Don of San Jose* has been my personal favorite. And today, the *Don of San Jose* show is rated number one in the universe."

"What show? What do you mean, you've been watching us? And what do you mean, the *Don of San Jose* show is rated number one in the universe? Are you an angel? Where did you come from?"

"All excellent questions Don," Blake replied. "But the answers are all big secrets here on Earth, can you keep a secret?"

"I'll try," Don replied. "No guarantees."

"At least you're honest," Blake said. "That's what I love about you Don. Well, you've heard of heaven, right? Everyone has, with pearls the size of houses and streets paved with gold?"

"Yes," Don said. "But I'm not dead."

"You will be, so listen up," Blake said, as he twirled and then pointed his stylus at Don. "Heaven isn't exactly like that. You see, when people die here on Earth, their soul goes to another planet somewhere in the rest of the universe. Some planets are better, some are worse. It's all totally fair, depending on how people handled their tests here on Earth.

"The surprise is, the universe is Earth-centric. We're all born into a body here on planet Earth, and then after our tests and we die, our soul goes to another planet somewhere in the rest of the universe. It's as simple as that."

"What if we fail our tests on Earth?" Don asked, thinking about reincarnation. "Do we get another chance?"

"Humans get up to thirty-three lives," Blake replied, "thirty-three tries to get it right and pass the tests on Earth."

"Limited reincarnation!" Don exclaimed, clapping his hands once. "That makes sense. People get thirty-three lives to learn to think of others first, otherwise they get burned with the chaff?"

"I told you Don! That's a big secret!" Blake said. "Please don't tell anyone on Earth, even Fonu, or I'll get in big trouble."

"Okay Blake, there's something I've always wanted to know. What do people do after they die? What does everyone do with all their time, on another planet, in the rest of the universe, for eternity?"

"We do whatever we want," Blake said, with a smile. "Because we learned it's better to do good things. It's not like on Earth, in human bodies, thinking about sex and survival all the time, which is enough to drive someone crazy. In the rest of the universe, we all create art. Everyone is an artist of some sort.

"The secret we learned was, there's plenty of time to learn new things. So, we just relax and have total confidence we can do it. We all paint, write stories, play music and thinks of others. Then, after work, we relax and eat something really good, just like it was on Earth. We go to shows and watch television. There's only one thing that's strictly forbidden."

"What's that?" Don asked.

"Watching Earth on television," Blake replied. "Everyone does it. It's everyone's favorite past time, but it's strictly forbidden."

"What?" Don said, with his eyes bugging out. "People who've died and gone to heaven, or another planet in the rest of the universe, can do whatever they want, but they choose to watch Earth on television? I can't believe it."

"Yes, I know, it is childish," Blake said, laughing. "But in the rest of the universe, people are so good most of the time, watching Earth on television is really our only guilty pleasure. We love watching the smartest people doing the stupidest things. We laugh until we cry. We remember how it was. We especially love you and Fonu, and all the good ideas you've had helping Dave.

"The whole universe loves you and your little group Don. That's why you're number one. You are so very loved. And we love the *Cult of Food and Dance Incorporated*. We love seeing fat people losing weight and dancing. We love your *Church in the Park* idea too, but what everyone's dying to know is, do you really love Donna? That's why *Don of San Jose* is rated number one in the universe today. The rest of the universe loves a good love story."

"So, the rest of the universe is on the edge of their seat, eh?" Don asked. "Everyone wants to know if I really love Donna, or if I'm just another man dog here on Earth, eh? Well, you know what Blake? I don't like the rest of the universe watching me and my friends on TV. What, are we being recorded right now? It sounds like you have cameras everywhere. Why don't you just read my mind too?"

"We can't read your mind Don," Blake said. "That was one of God's good ideas."

"Where are the cameras?" Don asked.

"We have flies, bees and gnats with nano-cameras and nano-phones literally everywhere," Blake said. "They have nano-computers interfaced to their insect brains. So, they can fly to a good spot and land, look and listen to anyone. They're perched all over your house right now. They're in your bedroom too. The rest of the universe saw you and Donna making love last night, and everyone wants to know if you really love her."

"I want to know if she really loves me!" Don said emphatically. "Can you tell me that?"

"That would take reading her mind Don," Blake said. "And I told you, we can't do that."

"If you can't read my mind, you'll just have to watch us on TV for the next seventy years or so. If you get my tone, I'm not too happy about you invading my privacy."

"Your so right Don," Blake said. "Between you and me and the flies, I think you really do love her. I'm so excited for you Don. Now, let's get you out of here."

"What?" Don asked. "You can get me out of here?"

"We can do almost anything Don," Blake said. "In addition to the insects, we have invisible flying robots of all shapes and sizes. And everything is being recorded, I mean everything. We can easily lift your DNA and make it disappear. And we can supply recordings of Donna explaining everything that happened to her. Once the police hear the story straight from her, you guys will look like the super-heroes you are, and you'll be in the clear."

"Well, get 'er done man!" Don said, with excitement and belief in miracles running through his veins again. He knew everything was going to be okay, and he was going to be with Donna again. "Mr. Blake, my friend from the rest of the universe, you're an answer to prayer."

"This time Don, your prayers had nothing to do with it," Blake said. "*Don of San Jose* is the highest rated show in the universe and you're the star of the show. Even a few angels watch every day. Everyone loves *Don of San Jose*. I'll take care of everything, I promise. I'll have you out of here in no time. Just remember, don't tell anyone about me, or the flies, or limited reincarnation, or anything. Anyway, they'll only think you're crazy," Blake said, laughing hysterically, and then he disappeared.

Blake arranged for Don's DNA to disappear, just as he promised. He also arranged for several videos to be delivered to the police. The videos proved Larry really did rescue Donna, and they showed that Don, Fonu and Dave helped her too. Other recordings convinced the detectives to turn their attention to Donna's father and his friend, who were now the perps under investigation.

CHAPTER 36

Don Gets Out

Detective Jensen came into the holding cell rubbing his chin, "Mr. Sanchez, somebody up there must like you. I received some recordings of you and your little cult friends. They showed a very good side of you. It's obvious, you and your friends were helping Donna. She doesn't seem crazy at all. And, it looks like you've been helping people lose weight too..."

At that moment, detective Jensen was interrupted as Captain Moss and Donna entered the room. Donna was smiling, which made Don's heart jump for joy. The Captain offered his hand to Don and said, "This whole thing started because I believed Donna's father right off the bat. I didn't question a thing he said, but I should have, especially seeing the cutting scars she had. I should've brought in a shrink immediately, and studied the case more deeply myself, but I believed him. I thought he was a loving father." Captain Moss lowered his head feeling ashamed. "I was lazy and swamped with work. I believed him only because we went to the same church. Now, I see how stupid that was. I have no idea where the recordings came from, but now I know the truth Don, and I admit I was wrong. You have my deepest apologies."

"That Captain, is the solution to world peace," Don said, smiling at Donna.

"World peace?" The Captain asked.

"Yes," Don said seriously. "Once we all can admit the possibility we might be one percent wrong, that's all we need to achieve world peace. And by we all, I mean, Catholics and Protestants, capitalists and communists, Muslims and Jews, and of course all parents, atheists, Buddhists and Hindus."

Then Detective Jensen said respectfully, "It was nice meeting you Mr. Sanchez." They both shook hands. Then he asked, "Do you think singing that song and dancing could help me lose a few too?"

"We'd love to have you Detective," Don replied.

"Don Sanchez, you are free to go," Captain Moss said.

Don took Donna's hand and they walked out bursting with gratitude.

CHAPTER 37

Big Church with the Stained-Glass Windows

Don and Donna came out of the building holding hands. Fonu, Dave, Zola, Gerry, and Abe were all there to greet them. "What happened Don?" Fonu Ali asked. "First, they said you were in big trouble. Then, they said you were being released."

"Give thanks for that," Don said. "Somebody up there must like me."

"Hey, guess what?" Donna said.

"What?" Fonu replied.

"It's my birthday today. Sorry I lied before. I really am eighteen now."

"You are eighteen," Don Sanchez said, as he took her right hand and looked in her eyes deeply. Then he dropped to one knee and said, "I love you Donna Davis. I want to be with you until we're old and wrinkled. Will you marry me?"

"Yes, I will," Donna replied, smiling wide and then kissing him.

"Let's get married this Sunday at nine, in the park," Don said. "We can get married and start *Church in the Park* on the same day. What do you think sweetie?"

"I want to get married in a big church with stained-glass windows," Donna replied, "like the big church next to the park."

"That's a Catholic Church," Don said, as he flashed back to the Catholic nun in the hospital, when he was fifteen and had his incredible healing. Then, he flashed back to how it was being raised by professors who didn't believe in God. All his anti-religious and anti-Catholic brainwashing was flashing through his mind too, as he gazed at Donna in her tight pink top. Don quickly concluded, he might possibly be wrong about the Catholic church being all bad. "Anything you want sweetie," Don said, as everyone watched them kiss gently. It was obvious they belonged together.

Gerry Long moved a step closer to Abe Seabrooke and whispered, "This is so big. We're going to have a wedding."

Abe moved a step closer to Gerry and held out his hand. Gerry looked at Abe, took his hand and said, "This is even bigger."

Dave was checking out Zola Jackson's ass. She turned around quickly, caught Dave's eye, and smiled. Zola felt good about her figure again. Dave smiled back, feeling good about Zola.

"I'll have a talk with the priest tomorrow," Don said. "I'll explain how I'm in love with a girl who wants to get married in a big church with stained glass windows. I'll also explain how, like Buddha, we have a problem with organized religion, and how, like Muhammad, we believe some church doctrine needs to change too. I'll explain how, after our honeymoon, we'll be going to *Church in the Park*, until the pope can agree he doesn't need to have the answer to everything. Then, we'll consider coming back."

Fonu was looking at Gerry and Abe holding hands. He had a scrunched-up look on his face like he was smelling something bad.

"Stop making faces Fonu!" Don exclaimed.

"Sorry Don. Hey, tell me what happened in there?" Fonu Ali asked, looking at Don intensely.

"I had the most incredible dream," Don said, as he observed a bee land on Fonu Ali's shoulder. "At least I think it was a dream. What do you think about limited reincarnation?"

Fonu Ali pushed his lips out for a moment and then said, "All human lives, or worms and insects too? You know I just can't accept becoming a bug or gnat or something."

"I don't know," Don said. "I didn't ask."

Epilogue

The next day, Don, Larry and Fonu went to the big Catholic church with the stained-glass windows next to the park. They talked with a priest and after twenty minutes of great conversation, Don felt they were on the exact same wavelength. They walked across the street to the park and strolled as they continued talking for two more hours. The priest agreed to perform the wedding under the radar, and he surprisingly agreed with Don's valid points about the problems with organized religion.

Don enjoyed getting to know the priest, and the priest really enjoyed getting to know Larry, Don and Fonu. The priest asked if he could be involved with *Church in the Park* too. He said it sounded like a really good idea.

Made in the USA
Las Vegas, NV
06 March 2023